MURDER AT THE HUNT BALL

A 1920S HISTORICAL COZY MYSTERY - AN EVIE
PARKER MYSTERY BOOK 10

SONIA PARIN

ISBN: 9798715373489

CHAPTER 1

Something's afoot

1921 - the dower house drawing room

"illie Leister. Now, there's a woman who knows how to get what she wants. After all, she managed to get all five daughters married off to titled gentlemen. If memory serves, one of those gentlemen did not possess a title but Tillie Leister managed to secure one for him…" Henrietta tilted her head in thought. "Does she owe me a favor? I'm sure she does. I seem to recall a ball in the spring of 1899 when she stepped on her ruffles and, losing her balance, she sent a priced vase toppling over. To this day, I have not revealed her secret to anyone."

Sara, the Dowager Countess of Woodridge, and Toodles, Evie's grandmother, stood at the entrance to the drawing room watching Henrietta holding up a dainty mirror and talking to her reflection.

Sara wanted to withdraw from the room and make her presence known by calling out or clearing her throat. But Toodles wrapped her hand around her wrist and stopped her.

It seemed Henrietta had a lot more to say and Toodles wanted to hear it.

"Then, there's Eleanor Bancroft." Henrietta nodded. "She has climbed every social ladder in existence and has a reputation for always knowing the right people." Henrietta chortled. "She knows me and I'm sure she has used that to her advantage. So, in a sense, she owes me."

In the next breath, Henrietta gasped and swung around. "Oh. I didn't realize I had an audience."

Toodles laughed and walked into the elegantly appointed drawing room. "We were waiting to see if the mirror spoke back to you."

Sara and Toodles settled down on a settee while Henrietta rose from her place at her desk and joined them.

"If you must know, I think I have developed a twitch," Henrietta explained. "I've been trying to catch myself in the act."

"A twitch?" Sara asked. "Are you feeling ill?"

"No, I'm perfectly fine. Except for the twitch. It has been catching me by surprise all morning. I suspect I twitched right throughout the night."

"What on earth is the matter with you, Henrietta?" Sara asked. "Should you see a doctor?"

Henrietta shook her head. "Oh, no. I doubt it is fatal. Only an inconvenience. Earlier, the Vicar dropped by and, I'm not entirely sure, but I think he now believes he is privy to a secret. My twitching seemed to bracket all my responses. I became so self-conscious, I didn't realize I'd lowered my voice."

Toodles laughed. "And he thought you were imparting a secret?"

"Yes, I believe so." Henrietta waved her hand. "He's rather absentminded. I'm sure he'll have forgotten all about it by now.'

Toodles and Sara leaned forward and studied Henrietta's eyes.

"Which one is it?" Toodles asked. "The left eye or the right eye?"

Henrietta looked concerned. "Oh, I don't know. They seem to be taking turns. Either that or they're playing a cat and mouse game with me."

"How often does it twitch?" Sara asked.

"I couldn't say with any certainty. I've tried timing it but it seems to be determined to keep me in suspense. Anyhow, I believe I am making some headway with our little project."

"Yes, we heard." Toodles sat back. "Apparently, you are in the process of calling in a few favors."

Henrietta looked slightly affronted. "Favors are not something I can take to my grave, so I might as well make the best of them while I can."

"So you're still determined to get Tom Winchester a title." Sara shared a whimsical smile with Toodles. "Some would say he deserves a title just for putting up with us."

Sounding defensive, Henrietta said, "I would hate to

think others might share your belief. We must put our heads together and find a way to get him a knighthood."

Sara gave her a small smile. "I hope you don't mean to involve the Royal family."

"I doubt we'll have to take such extreme measures. But I wouldn't discount it." Henrietta got up and rang for tea. "Have Tom and Evangeline set the date yet?"

"No, they're still being cagey about it. Although, I saw Birdie looking at a fashion magazine today, so she must be thinking about it."

"We can't plan anything without a date," Henrietta complained. "What about the reading of the banns? Oh, heavens. You don't suppose they will procure a special licence?"

"That might be just the way Birdie wants it," Toodles mused. Her granddaughter's first marriage to the Earl of Woodridge had been a grand affair. Perhaps too grand for Birdie's liking. It wouldn't surprise her if Birdie wanted to keep things simple by eloping.

Henrietta gave a firm nod. "I shall have to have a word with the Archbishop and encourage him to decline the request." She gave a pensive nod. "I believe *he* owes me a favor too."

Evie, the Countess of Woodridge, and Tom Winchester, the man who had been engaged as her chauffeur only to become a permanent presence in her life, had recently alluded to a possible engagement.

No one could say with any certainty if this had only been part of a gambit or if they were indeed headed down the aisle. Seth, the young Earl of Woodridge, had offered his congratulations but he hadn't been specific. For all anyone knew, he might have been congratulating Evangeline on a job well done assisting the police in their investigations.

Henrietta had set her heart on Evangeline, as she preferred to call her, marrying a titled gentleman. However, she had no intention of interfering in her choice. In any case, she rather liked Tom Winchester. Truth be known, she had been engulfed with a rising fear which she simply couldn't reason with. What if Tom took Evangeline away?

"Oh," Sara exclaimed. "I think I just saw your eye twitch."

"Which one?"

"Your right eye."

Henrietta patted her right eye.

"No, that's your left eye."

"My left eye is my right eye from where you are sitting."

"Yes, I suppose it is."

Bradley, Henrietta's butler, entered the drawing room and set the tea tray down on an intricately carved mahogany side table. He stepped back and, clasping his hands, he cleared his throat.

"Shall I pour?" Sara offered. "You might twitch at a most inopportune moment and burn yourself."

"I think I can manage it." Without looking up, Henrietta asked, "What is it Bradley?"

"My apologies, my lady. I do not wish to alarm you."

"And yet you have. Should I brace myself for bad news?"

"Not at all, my lady. It seems there have been a couple of clandestine meetings in the village and I thought you might wish to be informed."

"And now you want me to encourage you to release the rest of the information or do I need to coax it out of you by brutal force?"

"No, indeed, my lady." Bradley adjusted his sleeve. "The Countess of Woodridge and Mr. Tom Winchester have been meeting with a questionable looking person."

"Questionable?"

"One might say… dodgy, my lady." Bradley looked up at the ceiling. "The type of person one might encounter in a dark alley or in the dingiest, seediest streets of London."

Surprised, Henrietta asked, "In our village?"

Bradley nodded.

"Describe this person of dubious character."

Bradley cleared his throat again. "The details are sparse and, one might even say, contradictory. Some have described the person as scruffy. Others believe the person is a foreigner."

"Man or woman?" Henrietta asked, her tone a confusion of intrigue and surprise that such a character would be lurking in their quaint village.

"That too is hard to say, my lady."

"How can that be? It should be a simple matter of determining if the person in question is wearing trousers or a dress."

"Indeed, my lady. One would think so. However, some ladies have taken to wearing trousers and that makes the task of clarification difficult."

Sara and Toodles' attention bounced between Henrietta and Bradley, both expressing intrigue and delight at the exchange.

Henrietta's eyebrow lifted by tiny increments but it failed to have the desired effect. Instead of bowing and removing himself from the room, Bradley stood his ground.

"What else might one think? Meaning... what other information do you have at hand?"

Bradley gave it some thought. "To date, there have been several clandestine encounters."

"And for how long have these meetings been taking place?"

Bradley counted on his fingers. "Let me see... The first sighting occurred on Monday, today is Thursday. Four days, if you count Monday."

"And do these encounters occur at the same time and place? In other words, you need to provide details, Bradley. If I am to stir from the comfort of my drawing room, I need to be sure we will not be rushing into a wild goose chase."

"We?" both Toodles and Sara asked, their eyes brimming with amusement.

"My apologies," Henrietta said. "I should have been clearer. I am far too busy organizing a title for Tom. You should both set out as soon as Bradley gives you more detailed information."

"We should?" Sara asked. "Even if we're not the least interested in these curious meetings?"

"If you are not interested," Henrietta replied, "then why did you refer to them as curious?"

Sighing, Toodles looked at Bradley. "Henrietta makes a valid point. If I'm to trudge out, I'd like to know if I should head east, west, south or north."

Bradley gave a pensive nod. "I see. Well, the fact is, these meetings have been taking place all over the village."

Henrietta scoffed. "Lady Sara and Toodles cannot set

out to seek them here and seek them there. How do you come by the information?"

"It reaches me via several sources, my lady."

Henrietta's voice hitched and filled with disapproval. "You have spies in the village? And how do you receive this information?" She looked out the window and toward the quiet village beyond and had no trouble picturing people peering through keyholes or keeping observant eyes on everyone as they went about their daily business.

"Henrietta," Toodles chided. "We all know news travels. How it travels is a matter of practicality, resourcefulness and opportunity."

Henrietta lifted her chin. "I won't even pretend to understand what you just said."

"It's simple. As an example, a maid employed in a household on the edge of the village will not be able to abandon her post in order to rush here and inform Bradley of all the goings on in the village. She needs to be practical and find a way to convey the message without disrupting the household."

"I'm still in the dark. How is she resourceful?" Henrietta asked.

Toodles shrugged. "She might engage the aid of one of the other maids. That leads to her taking advantage of an opportunity and engaging the assistance of someone setting out to run an errand."

"Why didn't you say so in the first place?" Henrietta turned to Bradley. "How can you be sure the information hasn't been diluted?"

Bradley looked puzzled.

As she'd understood Henrietta's meaning, Toodles explained, "In the process of changing hands and making its way to you, the news might be exaggerated or distorted."

Understanding, Bradley nodded. "I believe the messages were relayed with expediency and brevity, my lady."

"And yet, we don't really know if Lady Woodridge has met with the same person or with several people on numerous occasions."

Bradley gave a hesitant nod. "That appears to be the case, my lady."

"Well, then. What are we to do?" Henrietta turned to Sara and Toodles.

"My granddaughter often appears to be spontaneous but she likes to think things through. We could wait and let Birdie tell us what is happening in her own time."

"By then, the ship might have sailed," Henrietta said.

"Oh," Sara exclaimed. "Do you think Evie is planning a voyage without us?"

"I did not mean it in the literal sense, however... She wouldn't. Surely, she wouldn't."

"Good heavens." Sara slid to the edge of her seat. "What if she is planning her honeymoon?"

Unperturbed, Henrietta said, "Planning her honeymoon? Do you think she has engaged the services of a person of dubious character to organize it all for her?" Henrietta scoffed at the idea. "In any case, I already have my clothes selected and I'm ready to leave at a moment's notice."

Sara relaxed. "I'm almost done with my packing."

Puzzled by the conversation, Toodles sat forward. "Are you both serious? Do you really expect to go on honeymoon with them?"

Sara and Henrietta nodded.

"Oh, absolutely. Knowing Evangeline, she will most likely run into some sort of trouble and we would like to be there to help her in any way we can."

Still surprised, Toodles asked, "When did you decide this?"

"I think we both came to the decision individually."

Sara nodded in agreement.

Henrietta looked up at Bradley. "Do you have an inside connection at Halton House?"

"I'm afraid not, my lady." Frowning, he added, "They are a tight lot."

"You should work on that, Bradley." Henrietta gave him a nod to signal he could leave. When they were alone, she turned to the others. "It really will be up to you to discover what Evangeline is up to. I'm afraid I'm busy pulling strings and planning how best to call in favors." Henrietta drummed her fingers on the armrest. "I believe I can rustle up a title for Tom Winchester but then... we'll have to give some thought to their situation. Of course, Evangeline will always outrank Tom Winchester and then there's the matter of, dare I say it, money."

Toodles scoffed. "You needn't worry about that. In fact, I believe, in that department, he outranks Birdie."

Henrietta and Sara gaped at her.

"My grandson confirmed it. That story about Tom striking it lucky in the Oklahoma oilfields is all true."

"Exactly how much is an oilfield worth?" Henrietta asked.

"A lot. And, before you suggest it, Tom would laugh at the idea of buying a title."

CHAPTER 2

A simple yes or no will suffice

A clandestine meeting
Somewhere in the village of Halton

"*I*t's a simple yes or no answer. I don't understand what is holding you back. Clearly, you want this as much as I do."

Evie brushed a finger across her chin. Four days of digging in her heels and putting off making a final decision. This had to be a record for her. "I understand this is time sensitive. However, there's a lot to consider. I wish I could give you a straight answer but my life is rather complicated. Such a commitment requires careful consideration."

And, Evie thought, yes or no answers were not always possible. For instance, did she like the color blue? The answer should be simple but it actually depended on the shade of blue in question.

Evie glanced at Tom's blue eyes.

She'd always thought of them as deep ocean blue, harboring great depth and mystery. She'd also heard the color referred to as indigo blue. Indigo. Deep ocean blue. It didn't matter what name it went by. She loved Tom's blue eyes. However, while the color reminded her of the ocean and Tom's eyes, it also brought back memories of her first tutor's indigo blue dresses. She'd been a hard taskmaster and quite liberal with her threats to withhold meals until her lessons were all absorbed.

Swallowing hard, Evie recalled the many lunches she had been forced to forego all because of her negligent attention span. So, since the color also made her think of hunger and punishment, she found herself in two minds and quite unable to provide a yes or no answer.

"You look confused."

Evie snapped out of her reverie and slumped back in the passenger seat.

Out of the corner of her eye, she could see Tom drumming his fingers on the steering wheel. And, she thought, staying right out of the conversation.

Glancing up, she looked at Lotte Mannering.

The lady detective had made a valid point. She did want to do this. She'd had four days to think about the offer. Why couldn't she decide and give her an answer right now?

She and Tom had been driving out every day to rendezvous with Lotte Mannering. Each day, Lotte had sported one of her many disguises making it difficult to spot her. Today, the lady detective had opted for a deranged look.

Her hair poked out from under her shabby looking hat. She wore glasses with thick lenses that made her eyes look bigger. Several layers of padding had added to her girth. The coat she wore looked threadbare, hung lopsided and had patches of various colors in the oddest places. For added effect, Lotte had been carrying two large hessian bags full of what appeared to be old rags.

"My apologies," Evie said. "I've been caught up with reminiscences. I will think about your proposal and I promise I will have an answer for you tomorrow."

Tom nudged her. "Someone's coming out of the store."

The 'someone' Tom referred to was the real reason for Lotte's regular trips to the village of Halton.

Lotte had described the young woman as tall with a mass of blonde curls.

"That's her," Lotte said.

"We'll talk tomorrow, I'm sure," Evie promised. "I expect you will telephone as soon as you set out this way."

Lotte Mannering nodded and, staying in character, she stretched her hand out. "Do you have a spare coin for an old woman, milady?"

Rolling her eyes, Evie dug inside her handbag, retrieved a few coins and handed them over.

The day before, Lotte had telephoned Halton House to alert them of her planned trip to the village of Halton. When they had driven out to meet her, they'd had to search up and down the main street several times before finally realizing they had driven past her almost as many times.

She had been dressed as a brawny farm laborer, complete with a rake and a spade. Today, they would have missed her again but when Lotte had seen them approaching, she'd waved them down.

"Let's head back," Evie said. "I should at least tell the others about the offer and hear their opinions. They're bound to have some."

The Countess of Woodridge, Lady Detective.

No, that didn't sound quite right.

Evie ran the phrase through her mind as Tom revved the engine and, with a wave to Lotte, took off.

"Lotte Mannering is becoming a master of disguise," Evie said. "I swear I didn't recognize her this time. Or, for that matter, any of the other times." The private detective had been staying at a nearby house and had trekked out to meet them in the oddest places, always dressed in a different disguise which, in Evie's mind, showed a great deal of passion for her profession.

As her private detective business had continued to expand and thrive, Lotte now felt it necessary to take on a business partner and she wanted someone she could trust.

How did she feel about becoming a private lady detective? The idea had been tossed around for a while, but she'd never really taken it seriously. Now Lotte had made a firm offer.

Evie knew she felt strongly about right winning over wrong, truth over lies. And, of course, she felt anyone who committed a crime should be brought to justice.

In her books, absolutely no one could claim they were above the law.

Tom leaned closer and said, "I agree with Lotte. It is a

simple enough question requiring a simple answer. Yes or no. It's your decision alone to make. No pressure."

Did she wish to go into business with Lotte Mannering? How would it impact her day to day life?

"I know you think I'm taking too long to decide but, as I've said, there's a lot to consider."

"If I had to guess," Tom said, "I'd say you've been busy looking at it from all angles and, in particular, from twenty or more years down the track."

"And you'd be right. This would be a long-term venture and, if I accept, it will have all sorts of repercussions. And then, of course, there is Seth to consider." The young Earl would forever be associated with a lady detective and a titled one at that.

Tom smiled. "I think Seth will love it. Every family should have an eccentric member."

"I see, I am to ultimately become the eccentric Countess. What other habits will you attribute to me?"

Tom grinned. "There'll be plenty of time to work on them."

Evie tilted her head in thought. "I'd have to be a silent partner."

He looked surprised. "You wouldn't want to flaunt it?"

"Absolutely not."

"Are you afraid of being snubbed by your society friends?"

Evie's voice sounded pensive, "Making it public would work against me. Lotte has her disguises. I could hide behind a mantle of… something or other."

"I think you meant to say respectability."

"Probably. As for my acquaintances… I think they would be intrigued and amused. But I would prefer to remain incognito. Yes, that would definitely work in my favor."

"There's no escaping the fact you are already associated with several cases."

"True. However, my involvement in those cases were all by chance. Anyhow, my greatest concern is about time. Lotte will expect me to drop everything and attend to cases."

"Would that be so bad?"

"I'm still the Countess of Woodridge. By now, you know that comes with a great deal of responsibility. The running of the estate has always been in capable hands but there are other matters to attend to."

"Tea parties and fundraisers?" Tom teased. "Maybe your cousin thrice removed could assist you."

Evie chortled. "Lady Carolina Thwaites? Yes, Caro would love that. But I'm sure she would prefer an active role in the detective business." Yes, indeed. Her maid would jump at the chance. "Heavens, I've just realized something."

"You haven't told her about Lotte's offer to become her business partner?"

Evie nodded.

"But you've known about it for four days. I thought you talked to Caro about everything."

"Only when I can get a word in edgewise." Evie groaned under her breath. "Henrietta, Sara and Toodles will feel left out. I'd never be able to hide it from them. Yes, we have to tell them."

Tom assured her, "On the bright side, you don't have to worry about me. I'm happy to go along with whatever you decide." Glancing at the envelope Evie held, Tom added, "At least you know Lotte is well organized."

Sighing, she drew out the piece of paper and read it. "Sterling Wright?" Lotte had been asking about him all week.

"What about him?" Tom asked.

"He's the one who engaged Lotte's services."

"Hang on. Aren't we attending a party or something thrown by him? Or are you still deciding?"

"Are you poking fun at me?" Evie nodded. "Of course, you are. And, yes, it's the Hunt Ball." Evie finished reading the case outline. "He engaged Lotte to shadow Miss Marjorie Devon, his fiancée. She's staying at his house, Hillsboro Lodge. And Lotte has been staying at the care-taker's cottage. When Miss Devon prepares to leave, Lotte receives a telephone call and she follows her. She doesn't say who calls her. I assume it's Sterling Wright."

"Does it say why he wants his fiancée followed?" Tom asked.

"Miss Devon has been receiving threatening letters and he's afraid she will come to harm."

"Since you received an invitation to the Hunt Ball, I assume you know Sterling Wright."

"Not really. I only met him once at the races. He's rela-tively new to the district. He has interests in horse racing and hails from our neck of the woods. A native New Yorker, he's been living in London and recently acquired Hillsboro Lodge. I suppose that's why he issued the invitation."

"Hillsboro Lodge. It sounds familiar. Where is it?"

"About a half hour drive south of Halton House."

"That's close. So why haven't we crossed paths with

him? Isn't that odd in these parts? Everyone seems to know everyone."

"Yes, yes, it is odd. I suppose he prefers to keep to himself. Or maybe he hasn't been spending much time in the country. Whatever the reason, it's about to change. I assume he's invited all the locals and this is his way of introducing himself."

"By locals, you mean the landed gentry and not the local washerwoman."

"Are you still poking fun at me? I've actually rubbed shoulders with the local washerwoman. Her name is Mavis Child. She's a widow. Last year, she won the blue ribbon for best fruit cake in the district."

Evie put away the letter. "Why would Sterling Wright pay Lotte to shadow his fiancée? Shouldn't he be more interested in finding out the identity of the person sending her threatening letters?"

"That's a very good question," Tom said. "You should ask Lotte tomorrow when you agree to become her business partner."

Evie glanced at Tom. She reached over and tipped his hat up slightly. "You seem to be eager for me to say yes."

"That's because I feel you really want to do this."

"What if I don't? Will you be bored with our life here?"

"Hardly. There's always something happening. I can't remember the last time I sat down to read in the library without some sort disruption dragging me away."

"Perhaps I should say no so that you can have your quiet time in the library."

He glanced at her. "And what will you do?"

"Work on those disruptions, of course."

They drove the rest of the way in silence. Evie

managed to suspend all thoughts about Lotte's offer. Instead, she focused on how she would share the news with Toodles and the dowagers.

She had no trouble imagining them wanting to become partners in the business. It would be a family affair.

The edge of Evie's eyes crinkled with amusement.

A family who played together and worked together… ended up in prison together or on the front page of a newspaper as proof of some scandalous behavior.

Could she keep her activities a secret from them? Toodles had been encouraging her to use her time more productively by taking up a profession. More recently, she had actively pushed her to join forces with Lotte Mannering. For all she knew, Lotte's offer had come as a result of Toodles' interference.

"I've decided I'm not going to tell them."

"Pardon?"

"I know I don't need their permission. Since I'm going to be discreet, I'd like to keep it all between us three. You, Lotte and myself. Make that four. Caro will need to know. Oh, and Edgar, of course." Her butler would never forgive her if she left him out. "In any case, I'm sure Toodles and the dowagers will figure it out and have fun in the process." Evie sighed. "Then again… they might interfere in the investigation. We saw what happened the last time we didn't keep them informed."

Tom laughed. "I love it when you argue with yourself out loud."

Evie huffed out a breath. "Not being able to provide a yes or no answer is plaguing me."

"Will Toodles and the dowagers be attending the Hunt Ball?"

"Yes, I believe so but I don't think Lotte meant for me to become involved in this case. After all, she is only following Miss Devon. How could I possibly help with that?"

"Well, she gave you the case outline and you did just raise the question of the threats and why Sterling Wright hadn't asked Lotte to look into them. Perhaps you could look into that."

And how would she do that? Evie tapped her finger on the envelope. "Before the Hunt Ball, there is the hunt itself. I suppose we could take part in the foxhunt. I hadn't planned on attending but we could go as spectators. There might already be some guests staying at Hillsboro Lodge."

Tom laughed. "You haven't made any firm commitments and you already suspect one of the guests."

"Yes, well… We have to start somewhere."

"By joining a foxhunt? I haven't seen you riding in a long time. In fact, I haven't seen you on a horse since we arrived at Halton House."

Evie shrugged. "It's all this business of sidesaddles. I'm accustomed to riding astride."

"And that is definitely out of the question for the Countess of Woodridge? I'm surprised."

Ignoring his remark, she asked, "Do you have a riding outfit?"

Tom grinned. "Of course."

It didn't surprise Evie. Since their arrival in England, Tom had been quite resourceful, showing a surprising ability to procure anything and everything he needed. He either knew how to cut a deal or, as she'd been suspecting all along, he really had struck it lucky in the Oklahoma oilfields. She'd been so blasé about his ability to suddenly produce a new car or full wardrobe she hadn't bothered to delve further.

Rather than suggest she might have changed her mind, she said, "We still have a few hours to decide if we'll join the hunt on horseback or on foot. As soon as we arrive at Halton House I will spend some time in the library making some notes. It would help to know who Miss Devon is."

"I bet you anything Henrietta will know something," Tom suggested. "She always knows who's who. What about Sterling Wright? What else do you know about him?"

"As I said, I only met him briefly. He's not much of a conversationalist. In fact, I suspect he doesn't even know much about horses. I don't remember hearing him talk about them."

"And what did he do to be able to afford to live here?"

She shook her head. "I'm surprised I don't know. Usually, that's the first thing we hear about a new person. Especially a foreigner. That's so and so from somewhere or other and he made his fortune in mining or the railways."

Tom mused, "A mystery man with a fiancée in peril."

"I wonder why Miss Devon is running around without a care in the world? Is she unaware of the threat? Or just reckless and carefree?"

"Lotte will be delighted by your curiosity and I think you want to impress her. This is definitely the right move for her. You see things from a different perspective. As they say, two heads are better than one."

"Why do you think she wants me as a partner? I mean, I could always just consult. This all sounds so formal. You don't suppose she needs a financial boost. She said her business is thriving. So, that can't possibly be the reason."

"She's in competition with another lady detective. Perhaps she sees this as a way to overtake her. With two of you, she'll be able to take on even more cases."

Evie thought about it and then shook her head. "No, she gave the impression she wants us to work together. She's cunning, so this might actually be a lure to rope me in."

"Brace yourself." Tom pointed ahead toward the entrance to Halton House and the dowagers' motor car. "Henrietta and Sara are here."

CHAPTER 3

Suspicious minds

The library, Halton House

"Did you notice anything unusual at lunch?" Evie asked.

"Are you still on the trail of suspicion? Actually…" Tom looked up from his newspaper. After a moment of thinking about it, he said, "Henrietta smiled a great deal. And, not her usual knowing smile. It was more of a brilliant smile. I think she might have been trying to distract us from her twitching eye."

"Her eye is twitching? I didn't notice."

Lunch with the dowagers and Toodles had been a

lively affair. Conversation had flowed and witticisms exchanged right along with knowing smiles.

Evie gave it some thought and then agreed with Tom. Henrietta's smile had been rather brilliant.

She supposed she hadn't really noticed because her attention had been focused on those exchanged smiles. They knew something and they were not bringing it out into the open. "They're up to something."

"So are we, Countess." Tom tapped his newspaper. "Sterling Wright is mentioned in an article about a new horse he purchased at auction. It went for a record price. That answers one question. He's loaded." He signaled to a stack of newspapers next to him. "Also, one of his horses placed in this year's Derby."

"I suppose that makes him a serious racing man. Was that ever in doubt?" Evie asked. "No, I don't think so. Then again, and I think I'm quoting myself, suspecting everything and everyone is a good place to start. The guilty do always hide behind a mantle of innocence."

"I could not have said it better myself." Tom set his newspaper down. "However, I doubt the thought would have occurred to me." Tom leaned back and looked up at the ceiling. "Actually, no real crime has been committed, so we have no reason to suspect Mr. Wright."

"True. I'm getting ahead of myself."

"And in the spirit of it all? I think you'll make a fabulous lady detective."

Evie hummed under her breath. "We might actually have reason to suspect him. Remember, he hired Lotte to trail after his fiancée but not to find out who is sending her threatening letters. I find those actions suspicious."

Tom smiled. "It's almost as if you're willing him to

commit a crime. I wonder if his fiancée has an interest in horses."

"Not all couples have shared interests," Evie mused and glanced at Tom. "I never asked. Are you interested in becoming involved in investigations?" He'd already expressed his enthusiasm for her involvement, but how did he feel about being dragged into chasing criminals?

"I most definitely am interested." He smiled. "You do make it interesting."

Evie tapped her fingers on the armrest. "I wonder if Toodles will be satisfied."

"Why wouldn't she be? She's been encouraging you to take an interest and pushing you in that particular direction."

"Yes, but… She'll probably wish me to become the *leading* lady detective. I'm afraid I'll find myself in competition right alongside Lotte. Knowing Toodles, she'll want to push me into crossing the ocean and expanding the business."

"That should be easy enough. Lotte already travels a great deal." Tom stood up and went to stand by the window. "Have you given any thought to the threatening letters Miss Devon has been receiving?"

"If I have, it doesn't necessarily mean I will be agreeing to become Lotte's associate. Will I need to work my social schedule around the business?"

Tom looked over his shoulder and gave her a raised eyebrow look.

"You know all my social engagements are planned in advance. If I'm suddenly dragged away, I'll have to explain my absence. Over time, I imagine I will come down with a multitude of ailments as an excuse for bowing out of a commitment. I'll be known as the malingering Countess." Evie looked toward the window. "I suspect Lotte will use me as a foot in the door associate."

"You're smiling."

"That's because the idea is beginning to take hold." Evie sat up and suggested, "We should drive up to Hillsboro Lodge and mingle."

"Get the lay of the land?"

"Yes. There are bound to be some early arrivals and everyone else taking part in the hunt." She leaned over and picked up the newspaper Tom had been reading. "Did you come across any photos of Sterling Wright? I can't remember what he looks like."

At the sound of voices approaching the library, they both turned toward the door.

Edgar walked in and tried to announce the arrivals but they simply barged in.

Lotte? Still dressed as a beggar woman...

Evie looked at the woman standing next to Lotte shoulder to shoulder and tried to place her. She looked familiar. After a moment, Evie remembered seeing her coming out of Mrs. Green's dressmaking establishment earlier in the day.

Miss Marjorie Devon, she presumed.

Lotte released her hold on the hessian bags she'd been carrying and crossed her arms. "Miss Devon, this is the Countess of Woodridge and this is Tom Winchester. Lady Woodridge... would you mind explaining to Miss Devon I mean no harm?"

Lotte's cheeks were flushed with red blotches and her lips pressed together so hard, they showed white at the edges. She looked out of breath. Her eyes, made larger by the spectacles she wore, danced around from side to side. Evie had trouble understanding the significance. Was Lotte trying to convey a message?

"I take it you need your identity confirmed."

"Yes. Please tell Miss Devon she has no need to contact the police." This time, Lotte's eyebrows bobbed up and down.

"Why does she wish to contact the police?" Evie asked.

"Because she thinks I'm responsible for sending her threatening letters. I have no idea what she's talking about." Lotte took a visible swallow and wailed, "I'm illegitimate."

"Illegitimate?"

"I can't even write."

"Oh, I think you mean illiterate."

Miss Devon harrumphed. "That's a likely excuse. You could get someone else to write the letters for you." The young woman smirked at Lotte. "This… This person is a *lunatic*. She's been following me all day long. It's clear she intends to do something to me. And, for all I know, you are her accomplice."

Miss Marjorie Devon stood a head taller than Lotte. Her tailored clothes looked disheveled. As she spoke, she shook her head. Evie watched her hat shift and slide off her.

"She kept screaming she's just a poor old woman trying to scratch a living," Marjorie Devon complained as she caught the hat and adjusted it in place.

Evie exchanged a knowing look with Tom. Clearly, Lotte hadn't given herself away and she wanted her identity to remain a secret.

"How exactly did you get here?" Evie asked. They were

within walking distance of the village, but she couldn't imagine them trekking out here in the middle of a dispute that threatened to involve the local constabulary.

"She chased me here!" Marjorie Devon declared, her voice rising to a high pitch. "Every time I tried to sidestep her, she cornered me. I thought she wanted to lead me to an alley where she could clobber me and rob me. Then she ended up herding me here. Yes, that's what she did. She *herded* me here."

Dragging two hessian bags? How had she managed it?

Edgar cleared his throat and lifted his chin. "My lady, I can confirm that. I first caught sight of them running across the park. Miss Devon clearly wished to escape but... this one here had her arms spread out as she screeched and roared like a deranged woman."

Instead of looking offended by the way Edgar had referred to her, Lotte appeared to be quite pleased with herself.

Miss Devon flung her arms out. "I abandoned my motor car in the village. Who knows if it will still be there when I return. What if she had an accomplice who drove away with it?"

Why had Lotte herded Miss Devon here? Did she have a specific plan in mind? If they were to become associates, she would have to learn to read Lotte's mind and interpret her prompts.

Pretending to be unaware of the full picture, Evie tried to look surprised and confused. Her tone remained calm as she said, "I don't understand how it could have happened. She's so much older than you. I'm sure you could have defended yourself."

Miss Devon's eyebrows drew down and she

demanded, "Is she who she says she is?"

Convinced Lotte wished to continue portraying herself as an indigent woman, Evie nodded. "As a matter of fact, she sometimes lives on the estate… in the hermit's hut. I can assure you, she is quite harmless. Although, sometimes, she goes on a rampage. Maybe that's what happened today. Maybe your accusations triggered it." Struck by inspiration, Evie added, "Loony Lotte, that's her name, is very sensitive to the slightest provocation. The poor, deranged woman was probably trying to seek refuge here and you misread her actions."

Marjorie Devon's eyes widened. "Are you saying this is my fault?"

Evie stood up. The young woman looked flustered and determined to have the matter resolved in her favor so Evie chose diversion as the best course of action.

"Miss Devon, I apologize for Loony Lotte's behavior. As she is my occasional guest, I feel responsible for her and I would hate for anything to happen to her. Would you allow us to drive you home or to the village to collect your motor car? I'm sure it's still there and no harm has come to it. Despite what you might think, this is a safe village."

Miss Devon appeared to think it over. "You need to control this woman. She is a threat to society."

Thankfully, Tom stepped in with a diversion of his own. "I'll get the motor car ready."

"Tom, perhaps you should get Edmonds to drive us and you can follow," Evie suggested.

Tom nodded and left to organize it.

Noticing Miss Devon was about to protest, Evie turned to Edgar. "Would you please show Loony Lotte to the kitchen and make sure she's fed and sent on her way? I'm sure she'll wish to spend some quiet time in the hermit's hut reflecting on the error of her ways."

Instead of protesting, Lotte huffed and, collecting her bags full of rags, she followed Edgar out.

Evie turned to Miss Devon and smiled. "I still find the idea of having a hut for hermits rather amusing. It's only when I came to England that I heard about the old practice. Before Loony Lotte took up residence, it had sat empty for a number of years. I suppose there is a scarcity of hermits…"

Miss Devon's brow furrowed and she gave a firm nod.

Interpreting this as a sign she meant to take up her cause again and demand some sort of satisfaction, Evie said, "I would offer you refreshments but you seem to be eager to return to your motor car." Evie excused herself and went to fetch a coat.

She could have sent for Caro, but she wished to avoid an encounter between her maid and Miss Devon. Caro, Evie thought, might be required to make an appearance at Hillsboro Lodge as her alter ego, Lady Carolina Thwaites, her cousin thrice removed.

As she came down the stairs, she found Miss Devon pacing in front of the fireplace in the hall.

Looking up, she gave Evie a tentative smile. "Lady Woodridge, I should apologize for my outburst. I've been on tenterhooks all week. Every time I came to the village, I had this overwhelming feeling someone was following me."

Lotte wouldn't be happy about that, Evie thought. She took great pride in the effectiveness of her disguises as well as her skills as a detective.

Why had Marjorie Devon continued to drive to the village? And why hadn't her fiancé told her about the measures he'd taken?

She had recently had a similar experience with Tom keeping secrets from her. At the time, she had been distracted by everything else going on in her life. However, she had made it clear she would never stand for such tactics again. Unlike other women who might have kicked up a fuss, she'd understood his reasonings. Still, she had made him promise he would never do it again.

"I didn't realize our little village held so many attractions," Evie said conversationally.

Marjorie Devon gave a small shrug. "Mrs. Green's dressmaking establishment is surprisingly good."

"Is Mrs. Green making clothes for you?" Evie asked as they stepped outside and walked toward the waiting Duesenberg.

"I already have my trousseau organized," Marjorie Devon explained. "Oh, did I mention I am engaged? No, I don't suppose I did. Anyhow, one can never have too much. In truth, I'm afraid I'm not an enthusiastic country person. Everyone staying at Hillsboro Lodge is keen to ride. I don't mind it but it seems too much when you're expected to go out every day."

"So you escape to our little village," Evie offered.

Marjorie nodded. "It is quaint."

Edmonds held the door open for them. Settling into the back seat of the Duesenberg, Evie glanced over her shoulder and saw Tom ready to follow them in the roadster.

As they drove off, Evie gave Miss Devon a worried smile. "My apologies for Looney Lotte's behavior and thank you for not reporting her to the constabulary. It is very decent of you. She's had a very difficult life."

Marjorie Devon shifted in her seat. "Yes, well... I suppose one must do what one can for her sort. Although, why she is allowed to roam freely is beyond me. She is a danger to society."

Evie offered her an encouraging smile. "I hope this doesn't stop you from coming to our lovely village."

Marjorie Devon persevered, "Someone should do something about her."

Evie assured her, "I'll do my best to get through to her."

"Yes, please do. I still have a couple of fittings at Mrs. Green's and I don't want to be looking over my shoulder."

"I'll be happy to accompany you," Evie offered.

"Oh, that's kind of you but I prefer to go alone. It's the only time I seem to have to myself."

Evie gave her an understanding smile. "I might see you there at some point. Mrs. Green is making me a dress for the Hunt Ball and I have an appointment for a fitting." Evie made a mental note to contact Mrs. Green and inform her of her plans.

Marjorie Devon's brows wrinkled with concern and focus. Her eyes narrowed slightly. Evie watched as Miss Devon appeared to debate a major issue. She hoped the young woman wouldn't insist on reporting Lotte's antics.

She continued to frown and stare fixedly ahead.

Evie set her age at twenty-five, perhaps younger. Too young to have any significant concerns weighing her thoughts.

From one moment to the next, Marjorie Devon's worried look evaporated and she gave Evie a bright smile.

"I had a new dress made especially for the ball. But Mrs. Green has enticed me with a new one and now I'll have to decide which one to wear. I only hope I don't clash with another guest."

"You can at least avoid clashing with a guest staying at the house by sending your maid on a spying mission," Evie suggested.

She seemed to like the idea.

"Have any of the guests arrived?" Evie asked.

"Yes, most of the avid riders who live in town. Sterling has a splendid stable. Although, some have brought their own mounts. The rest of the guests are trickling in."

"Do you ride?"

"Occasionally, yes. It depends on the weather. I hate going out when it drizzles. It does my hair no good."

Seeing Edmonds driving at an unusually slow speed, Evie wondered if Tom had suggested it so she could take advantage of their brief time together and question Miss Devon.

"I wonder if I'll know anyone," Evie mused. "I met your fiancé once, but only briefly."

"I'm sure you'll know most of the local people. Then, there's Twiggy Lloyd. He has already settled in. He arrived the day before yesterday."

"I'm afraid I don't know him."

"He's a racing enthusiast. Despite his name, he's quite robust. He came with his wife, Helena." Marjorie Devon tapped her chin. "Then there's Matthew Prentiss and his wife, Pamela. Archie Arthurs came alone. They are all involved in horse racing. Sterling says this ball is my opportunity to become acquainted with the locals." She gave Evie a pointed look.

"You'll have an interesting story to tell about our first encounter." Evie cleared her throat and broached the subject uppermost in her mind. "Why did you think Looney Lotte wrote you threatening letters?"

Marjorie Devon bounced on her seat and pointed ahead. "Oh, thank heavens. There's my motor car."

Edmonds slowed down and parked behind the little roadster.

Evie waited for Marjorie Devon to respond. When she didn't, Evie made a mental note to look into Miss Devon's background. Why would someone send her threatening letters and how many had they sent... and what did they say?

As soon as Edmonds opened the door for her, Marjorie rushed out saying, "Thank you, Lady Woodridge. You have been most kind."

Evie called out, "Tom and I will follow you back to make sure you arrive safely." Evie had to move fast. As she hurried toward the roadster, she called out, "Thank you, Edmonds. Mr. Winchester will drive me back."

When she settled in the passenger seat, Tom laughed. "Follow that roadster?"

"Yes. My heavens." Evie adjusted her hat. "She's in a hurry to get away."

Tom glanced at her. "From the village, from the awkward experience with Loony Lotte or from you?"

Staring straight ahead, Evie said, "That woman is up to something."

"Does this mean you're officially on the case?"

"Yes." In the next breath, Evie laughed. "I wish I'd seen Lotte chasing Marjorie Devon across the park."

CHAPTER 4

Hillsboro Lodge

om and Evie raced through the countryside with Marjorie Devon whizzing past the gates to the estate ahead of them.

Tom managed to keep up with her so they were able to see her bringing her roadster to a screeching halt in front of the entrance to Hillsboro Lodge where a footman promptly appeared to greet her.

Evie had never visited Hillsboro Lodge. The gray stoned manor house faced a lake and a park with visible trails weaving around it. It appeared to be a sizeable estate —a testament to Sterling Wright's wealth.

"Are we inviting ourselves in?" Tom asked.

"Let me catch my breath. Heavens, I'm accustomed to your fast driving but Miss Devon is a daredevil behind the wheel. I've never seen such reckless driving."

Marjorie Devon had skidded a couple of times but had managed to get the motor car under control. The near misses had not stopped her from dashing off at a mad pace.

"We might be in luck." Tom signaled ahead. "It looks like she's alerting the footman to our presence. Then again, she might be asking him to contact the local constabulary because she's been chased by a couple of lunatics."

"Mr. Winchester, you have a wild imagination."

"I'm trying to fit in." Tom leaned forward and looked across the park. "Hello, what's that?"

Evie followed his gaze.

They saw a man dismount and march toward another man on a horse.

"He's not at all pleased. He's stomping toward the other rider," Evie observed. "Is he waving his whip?"

Tom agreed, "They're definitely having words."

"Twiggy Lloyd doesn't look at all happy."

"How do you know his name?"

"I'm guessing. Marjorie Devon described him as robust. I'm inclined to amend it to rotund. He is rather chubby."

"And yet, he looked quite agile dismounting the horse."

"True."

They continued to watch them. Even from a distance, they could see they were arguing; their aggressive posturing included fisted hands, finger pointing and even the brandishing of their whips.

"It's now beginning to feel awkward," Evie murmured. Were they witnessing an ongoing dispute or the result of some sort of mishap on the field? They'd already seen

Miss Devon home safely. Should they move on or wait to see if they were invited in?

"I hope you're not about to suggest I try to intervene. I'd either have to clamber all the way up that hill or drive up. I'm sure Sterling Wright won't enjoy having his lawn ruined with track marks."

The argument came to an end when the rider trotted toward the house. When he reached the courtyard, a groom rushed up and assisted him by taking the reins.

The man dismounted and walked toward Marjorie Devon. Leaning in, he kissed her cheek.

"That must be Sterling Wright." And he had been arguing with Twiggy Lloyd.

Tom nudged her. "Marjorie Devon is telling him about us. She keeps looking toward us and she looks worried."

"That could mean anything. She might be worried about making a bad impression." As she spoke, Evie kept her eyes on Twiggy Lloyd. "She could be saying they should invite us in for a cup of tea to make up for her transgression. Remember, she accused me of being in cahoots with Loony Lotte."

"But you are."

"She doesn't know that."

"Well, she's doing a lot of talking and he's just listening."

"My kind of man," Evie teased.

"They're coming." Tom jumped out, rounded the motor car and opened the door for Evie. "Stop looking at Twiggy Lloyd and put on your charm."

"For your information, I never switch it off."

Sterling Wright approached them and greeted them with a bright smile. "Lady Woodridge. What a pleasant surprise. Marjorie has just told me what you did for her. I am in your debt."

A slim man in his mid-thirties, his angular features, including a sharp nose, gave him a severe look. However, when he smiled, his face lit up.

Evie introduced Tom and, as hoped, Sterling Wright invited them in for refreshments.

As they stepped inside the house, Evie heard the crunch of footsteps on the gravel.

Turning, she saw Twiggy Lloyd leading his horse. He handed the reins to a groom and made his way inside.

Sterling noticed him. Stopping, he made the introductions.

If there were any ill feelings between the two men, they did not show it. Despite the fact they'd just been arguing, Evie didn't pick up any awkwardness between the two men.

After a polite exchange, Twiggy Lloyd excused himself saying he needed to freshen up.

Sterling Wright led them through to a large library where the footmen were just finishing setting up.

Everyone helped themselves to tea and made small-talk about the view and the weather.

They heard some other guests returning from their ride. Evie braced herself for the introductions, but they all made their way directly upstairs.

"It was an informal ride," Sterling explained. "We went out with the hounds earlier today. I do hope you'll join us tomorrow."

Marjorie Devon took a quick sip of her tea, set her cup down and excused herself saying, "I really need to change out of these clothes and I feel the heel of my shoe is about to come off. They were certainly not made for running."

Evie wondered how much Marjorie had told Sterling. Also, she wished she knew if Lotte had told him about her disguises. If he knew about them, he might be prepared to brush off Marjorie's complaint allowing Lotte to continue with her investigation.

Sterling Wright didn't appear to be in a hurry to see them on their way, so Evie took the plunge and mentioned the threatening letters.

"How did you hear about them?" Sterling asked.

"Your fiancée mentioned them when she accused Looney Lotte of sending them."

Sterling Wright nodded. "Marjorie mentioned her encounter with a beggar woman."

Evie didn't know if she should mention it had actually been Lotte.

"Looney Lotte." Sterling smiled and shook his head. "It can't be a coincidence."

"What do you mean?"

To her surprise, he mentioned hiring Lotte. "She's supposed to be discreet," he said. "I had no idea what measures she would take."

That answered her questions. However, Evie decided to avoid any mention of her association with Lotte, at least until she'd spoken with her and sorted out the details. "Can you think of any reason why someone would target your fiancée?"

He looked down at his cup of tea. "No, not unless they're using her to get to me."

"And why would someone do that?"

He chortled. "Any number of reasons. I have significant interests in the racing world. It's possible I might have upset someone."

"In what way?" Evie asked, her tone conversational.

He shrugged. "I can't really imagine. I only know I'm involved in a highly competitive arena."

Evie remembered Tom mentioning the purchase of a horse at auction. Maybe Sterling Wright had outbid the wrong person.

He looked pensive. "It can't have anything to do with racing. The season is over. Otherwise, I might imagine someone wanted to distract me."

"What do you mean? Distract you from what?"

"I like to involve myself in the training of the horses. If I'm distracted, it could impact the outcome of a race."

Evie tried to think of another angle they might explore. "When did Miss Devon start receiving the letters?

He didn't have to think about it. "About two weeks ago."

"Can you think of anything significant that might have happened at about that time?"

He looked at her for a long moment and then set his cup down. "I purchased a horse, Mighty Warrior." He looked worried and after a moment he smiled. "No, this can't have anything to do with my horses."

～

An hour later...

. . .

Sterling Wright had guided the conversation away from the letters, spending a considerable amount of time convincing Evie and Tom to join in the hunt.

Saying she would have their horses sent over the next day, they excused themselves and returned to Halton House.

Tom waited until they arrived to ask, "Well, what did you make of all that?"

"The first thought that comes to mind?"

Tom nodded.

"Sterling Wright told us a great deal without telling us anything." He had to be an astute man and yet he hadn't made the connection between the purchase of a new horse and the start of a campaign of threats.

Edgar met them at the door and took their coats and gloves.

"I hope we're not late." Evie looked at her watch. "Oh, it's nearly time to change for dinner."

Edgar nodded. "I was about to ring the gong, my lady. The dowagers arrived five minutes ago and..." he cleared his throat. "Loony Lotte is still here. She wonders if someone could drive her back to the village where she left her motor car. As she wishes to remain inconspicuous, she would like to wait until dark. Of course, that means she also wishes to be fed again."

"And where is she now? With the dowagers and Toodles?"

"Yes, my lady."

Edgar's willingness to play along and adjust to unex-pected circumstances never ceased to surprise Evie.

Evie made her way to her room to change for dinner

saying, "I suppose we have no choice but to let them in on the case."

She walked into her bedroom, her thoughts filled with everyone's odd behavior. Had she misread the situation? Why should she expect Sterling Wright to respond to her intrusive questions with detailed replies? She'd been lucky he'd given her any sort of reply.

Evie found Caro examining a gown. After the eventful morning she'd had, she looked forward to a relaxing chat. Eventually, she thought, she'd tell Caro about Lotte's proposal and watch her maid's reaction. Evie knew Caro would be excited by the prospect of possibly playing the role of her cousin thrice removed.

"Hello, Caro."

"Milady! I wondered when you'd come up. I've been fretting all afternoon. No one will tell me anything. When I found Looney Lotte in the kitchen, I immediately knew you'd be working a case."

Caro looked flushed with excitement.

"Didn't Lotte fill you in?"

"No, in fact, she stayed in character the whole time. At one point, she even became hysterical and tried to pull her hair out."

Amused by the mental image that formed in her mind, Evie sat at her dressing table and removed her earrings. "I'll be needing my riding clothes tomorrow, Caro. The breeches, not the skirt."

Caro gasped.

Evie didn't give her the opportunity to express her opinions. "Do you ride?"

"Me, milady? Heavens, no. I tried it once but I lost my breakfast."

"In that case, you'll have to get your tweeds out. We'll need Lady Carolina Thwaites to make an appearance."

Caro gasped again and Evie thought she heard her say, "This is too much."

Stumbling back, Caro eased down onto the edge of the bed.

"Caro? Are you crushing my evening gown?"

Jumping to her feet, Caro smoothed out the dress.

Glancing at her maid's reflection in the mirror, Evie said, "You might as well know I am giving serious thought to joining Lotte's lady detective agency."

Gasping yet again, Caro once again lowered herself onto the bed.

"Caro, are you coming down with something?"

"A case of shock, milady."

"You're surprised?"

"I should have known something was about to happen when the dowager asked me to accompany her tomorrow."

"Which one?"

"Lady Henrietta."

Evie's eyebrow curved up. "Where is she going?"

"She wants to follow the hunt."

It was Evie's turn to gasp. "Henrietta? On foot? As a spectator? Following the hunt?"

"I found it odd too, milady. And then, your mother-in-law and Toodles said they would be going along too."

"Did they say why?"

"I only heard part of the conversation. Apparently, they mean to get to the bottom of something."

Heavens, what could that possibly mean? "Did they decide this after they heard about Looney Lotte?"

Caro nodded.

"That makes sense," Evie murmured.

Having recovered from her shock, Caro helped Evie change into her gown. "So what will Lady Carolina be expected to do?"

"Mingle and listen. I'll tell the host you arrived by surprise. He'll understand I couldn't leave you behind."

A light knock at the door was followed by Lotte's entrance. She still wore her costume and looked quite comfortable in it.

"You have a lot of explaining to do," Evie said.

Lotte groaned. "There's no time for that. I have until tomorrow to work out another strategy. Miss Devon will be more vigilant now."

"How did she ever find you out?"

Lotte rifled through a small box of trinkets almost as if she needed a part of her to remain in character. "I expected her to go home straight after her dressmaking appointment. Instead, she lingered in the village. Then, she went inside the tearooms. I hovered nearby and I might have peered through the window a couple of times. Anyhow, she must have gone out the back door. Next thing I knew, she crept up on me and accused me of following her."

"Yes, but how did you both end up here?" Evie tried to picture the scene with both women crossing the small memorial park and then dashing through the lane and into the open field. The Halton House estate bordered the village. Despite that, there were still the open fields to traverse. It would have been quite a hike.

"I couldn't give myself away so I started acting like a

mad woman." Lotte grinned. "I sort of got carried away. In fact, I found it rather liberating."

"And no one came to her rescue?"

"A few people looked out of their windows. That's when I decided to steer her toward Halton House."

Evie shook her head. "I still don't understand how Miss Devon allowed herself to be herded here. In her place, I would have tried to find shelter in one of the premises. Anyhow, I suspect it all worked out in your favor. You have me cornered now. I have no choice but to step in and do my bit."

Lotte picked up a pair of earrings. Holding them up to her ears, she walked up to stand behind Evie and used the mirror to study her reflection and admire the earrings. "I hope you befriended Marjorie Devon. She's bound to go into the village again and I'll have to keep my distance. You could accompany her or… you could bump into her by accident."

Evie shook her head. "I've already suggested that. She says she prefers to go alone. I considered visiting Mrs. Green's establishment. But, I can't do it tomorrow because Tom and I will be at the hunt."

"You're riding?"

Evie made her mind up on the spot. "Yes, why are you so surprised?"

"I suppose I could be a spectator and come as myself. I need to see this with my own eyes."

"What about Marjorie? I doubt she'll ride. You'll have to find some other way of following her. Although, perhaps Sterling Wright should suggest she stay at the house for the time being." Standing up, Evie turned her attention to finishing dressing for dinner. When she finished, she sat down again to let Caro work on her hair. "By the way, what's in the letters she received? I tried to ask Sterling but he changed the subject."

"He only showed me one letter." Lotte sat on the edge of the bed and picked at one of the patches on her coat. "It cut straight to the chase saying Marjorie Devon would pay."

"How was it phrased?"

"You'll pay big time."

What had she done to earn someone's ire? "What do you know about her?"

"She comes from a good family. No title. Her father works in banking. They've always lived in town. She's been engaged before but he perished in the war."

Evie gave a small shake of her head. "The surplus two million," she whispered. Just after the war, there had been an estimated one million women destined to a life of spinsterhood because so many men had been lost. Then, recently, the Census had been published and the figure had doubled. Newspapers had unkindly dubbed them the 'superfluous women' destined to lead unfulfilled lives as if marriage alone could provide them with an acceptable, useful role in life. Books were being written about the problem, focusing on the far-reaching consequences. One woman, at least, wouldn't have to worry.

Evie had noticed the age difference between Marjorie Devon and Sterling Wright. Had she settled for what she could get? Some women would find a second-best choice better than no choice at all.

Glancing at Caro she worried her young maid might have missed out on finding a husband. She knew Caro had dreams of someday marrying. Broadening her horizons, Evie thought, would certainly increase her chances. She could definitely do something about that, even at the risk of losing her.

"How did Marjorie Devon meet Sterling Wright?" Evie asked.

"At a charity event."

Evie couldn't help expressing the first thought that came to mind. "Did she steal him away from someone else?"

Caro growled softly.

"What is it, Caro?" Evie asked.

"Why do you assume she's at fault?"

"I don't. At least, I don't believe I assumed. It's just a possibility. She is strong-minded. And I'm trying to think of reasons why someone would send her threatening letters." Evie shrugged. "She strikes me as the type who enjoys having her way. For instance, she's staying at her fiancé's house but instead of enjoying the entertainment and mingling with the guests, she goes off by herself because country sports don't hold her interest. It makes me wonder what she has in common with Sterling Wright."

"Yes, and there's a significant age difference," Lotte offered. "He appears to be in his early forties."

"Mid-thirties, I think." Evie sighed. "If we can't follow her, we might have to find a way to stay at the house without anyone suspecting."

"That leaves me out," Lotte said. "Sterling Wright would recognize me straightaway and I'm sure Marjorie Devon would too, even if I put on my best disguise."

Evie gave a firm nod. "It'll have to be me."

"How will you manage it, milady? You live so close to the house, you can't use distance as an excuse."

"I'm going riding tomorrow. I could have an accident."

Caro gasped and gave a fierce shake of her head. "Milady. No."

"It wouldn't be real. I could pretend I've come off my horse and... sprained my ankle." She tilted her head in thought. "Would that be credible enough?"

Lotte shook her head. "Tom Winchester should be able to drive you back home."

"True. Then, I'll have to suffer an injury that won't allow me to travel."

Caro went pale. "That is asking for trouble, milady. I'm not sure I can allow that."

"Thank you for your concern, Caro. But I can assure you nothing bad will happen to me. I will only be pretending to be injured."

"And how will you attend the ball?"

"I will have recovered by then."

Caro shook her head. "I don't see it working in your favor. The whole point to you being there is to be close to the guests, but they will be out and about riding and you will most likely be convalescing in your room."

Evie exchanged a look with Lotte. "I hadn't thought of it that way. We'll have to think of something else. They'll be riding every day until the ball which marks the end of the foxhunting season." Evie shuddered. "Poor fox."

Lotte groaned. "Please don't get it into your head to liberate the fox."

"Why would I do that?"

"Because you have been known to do strange things."

"Then why are you so keen for me to join your lady detective agency?"

"Because sometimes your unconventional, strange ideas get results."

"I'll take that as a compliment." Evie rose to her feet. "I believe we have no other option. We must recruit the dowagers and Toodles. But, first, I'll need to make a telephone call."

CHAPTER 5

Bright-eyed and bushy-tailed

Hillsboro Lodge
The next morning

om complimented Evie, "You look very fetching in your riding breeches."

"As do you."

Whistling, he brought the roadster to a stop. Ahead, near the front entrance to Hillsboro Lodge, the riders were already congregated, some already mounted on their hunters, others mingling while footmen were busy distributing drinks and fruit cake. The hounds were running around yapping with excitement as they sensed the thrill of the chase.

Evie lifted her chin. "Before we go on, I would like it to go on the record that I disapprove of the idea of chasing after a poor fox. And that is all I'm going to say on the subject but I will do my best to enjoy a good gallop without breaking my neck." Evie cringed. "Please stop me if I try to intervene and rush to the fox's rescue."

She recognized the Halton House stable hand sent over with the Woodridge hunters. "Billy's waiting for us, so I suppose there's no putting this off any longer or changing my mind."

"Countess, just don't go jumping over fences or hedges or anything higher than a blade of grass. I'm still responsible for you," Tom warned.

Evie grinned. "Brace yourself, I'm going to give you a good run for your money."

As she greeted Billy, she saw the dowagers, Toodles and Caro arriving in the Duesenberg. They were all dressed in their warm country tweeds and looked quite thrilled to be there. Clearly, Lotte had decided to stay away.

Caro fussed with her hat and tried to keep up with them as they walked around inspecting the horses.

Taking the reins, Evie greeted her horse, "Hello, Poppy. It's been a while so you'll have to be patient with me."

"What's my horse's name?" Tom asked.

"Oh, that's Clover."

"I'm riding a weed?"

"Clover isn't a weed. It's a herbaceous plant. We give all our horses plant and flower names."

"I suppose I shouldn't complain. I could have been riding Daisy."

"Ah, this is about your manhood." Evie turned and signaled to Billy who promptly produced a block for her to step on. She took hold of the reins and, with her foot firmly in the stirrup, she heaved herself up. "Good girl, Poppy."

Tom mounted Clover and walked up to Evie. "If you're harboring any second thoughts, now is the time to speak."

"Or forever hold my peace? Well, I haven't come up with a feasible plan so we'll just have to play it by ear." When she'd told Tom about her idea to fake an accident he'd immediately vetoed it, echoing Caro's sentiments and saying it would be tempting fate.

"I'm actually worried about Henrietta. How is she going to manage all the walking? In my experience, not all the tracks are made for walking. That's usually the case in most estates."

Tom laughed. "There's your answer."

"Pardon?"

"Look over there."

Evie turned and saw Billy leading a donkey and cart. "She wouldn't. Surely, she wouldn't."

They both followed Billy's progress. When Henrietta saw the stable hand approaching, her smile widened.

"I hear Queen Victoria enjoyed riding around in one of those," Tom said.

She should not have been surprised to see Billy run off and return with yet another donkey and cart.

"You look annoyed," Tom observed.

"I am, but only because they managed to come up with a solution to a problem."

"Without your assistance?"

Evie gave a reluctant nod. "Not only that. I actually doubt I would have thought of the idea."

"Lady Woodridge." Sterling Wright steered his horse toward them. "I'm so glad you decided to join us."

"And I'm glad I came. Although, I'm sure my opinion will differ tomorrow. I haven't been riding in a while." Trying to identify the people staying at Hillsboro Lodge, she pointed at a man and said, "I don't recognize him."

"That's Archie Arthurs. This is his first hunt."

He looked stocky and, even if Sterling Wright hadn't mentioned it, she would have known he had limited experience on horses. His shoulders were stooped and his slouching posture left a lot to be desired. In fact, the man didn't look at all confident and his horse looked skittish.

A man and a woman sidled up to Archie Arthurs and appeared to share a joke as they all laughed.

"That's Matthew Prentiss and his wife, Pamela." Sterling Wright leaned in and said, "You made quite an impression on my fiancée. The moment she heard you'd be riding, she rushed off to organize herself." He lowered his voice and added, "To be quite honest, I never thought she'd take to country pursuits. I almost regretted purchasing this property. In fact, I'd been thinking of selling up and returning to town."

His consideration surprised Evie. It showed a desire to share some interests and make his fiancée happy. Then again, she shouldn't be surprised since he'd taken measures to look after her safety by hiring Lotte to follow her.

"Here she is." Sterling tipped his hat and greeted Marjorie Devon with a warm smile.

The veil on the young woman's hat covered half her

face but Evie could sense a forced smile on the young woman who actually rode sidesaddle.

"Lady Woodridge. How I envy you. Perhaps I should consider riding astride. It's a shame I wouldn't be able to wear this lovely outfit."

Evie smiled and was about to reply when the master of the hunt blew his horn. A slight moment of confusion and a burst of excitement ensued. Then, suddenly, everyone took off after the hounds. The field followed with various degrees of enthusiasm, with Evie and Tom lagging behind.

Evie searched the riders and located Twiggy Lloyd, his rotund body making the search quite easy. A woman rode beside him and they appeared to be engaged in an animated discussion.

As Marjorie Devon had mentioned Twiggy's wife, Evie searched her memory until she remembered the woman's name. "Helena Lloyd."

After a moment, the woman leaned forward slightly, encouraged her horse, and took off. Twiggy Lloyd smacked his hand on his thigh making his displeasure all too obvious.

"Are we bringing up the rear on purpose?" Tom asked. "Or are you about to bow out of the hunt?"

"There's no hurry. I think it will give us a vantage point. We can observe everyone. As I said, I haven't been on a horse in a while so it might be best to ease into it." Although, she knew the precaution wouldn't stop her from lamenting the day.

They continued on at a gentle canter and almost lost sight of the field.

"We risk being labeled lethargic," Tom remarked. "And

54

I think Clover is getting ideas about stopping for a bite to eat."

"Oh, heavens, anyone would think you enjoy complaining." Evie gave Poppy a light encouragement and she took off at a gallop. Smiling, she called out over her shoulder, "There, are you happy now?"

It took a moment for Tom to respond. When he did, he had no trouble catching up to Evie.

So much for Marjorie Devon's lack of interest in country pursuits, Evie thought as she observed the young woman galloping at breakneck speed and having no trouble keeping up with the rest of the field.

She glanced toward her left and saw the dowagers, Toodles and Caro making their way along a track that rose up alongside the open field. Either they knew precisely where they were going or they were merely following the other spectators.

Evie loosened her hold on the reins slightly and relaxed into the ride. They were now narrowing the gap and catching up to the field of riders which had slowed down.

"The hounds look confused," Evie shouted.

"They're just trying to pick up the scent," Tom hollered.

They finally caught up with the rest of the field. Evie and Tom slowed down again. They could see the hounds were frantic with excitement, their noses to the ground as they tried to identify the right scent. They almost looked discouraged. Then one of them gave a determined bark and took off with all the others following on its trail.

Evie barely had time to catch her breath. As she looked

up and tightened her hold on the reins, she noticed Marjorie Devon looking over her shoulder at her.

"What's the plan this time?" Tom asked. "Do we keep up or follow at a discreet distance?"

Poppy danced from side to side while Tom's hunter, Clover, stood perfectly still.

"Poppy's eager to follow. So… Giddy up." Before Tom could respond, Evie took off.

She galloped across the open field, with Tom fast on her heels. Glimpsing over the rise, she saw the little carts making their way along. Somehow, Henrietta had managed to gain an even better advantage as the higher ground offered her a perfect view of the foxhunt in progress.

Tom and Evie followed the field down a slope and caught up with them just as the riders galloped alongside a brook.

"Argh!" Evie screeched when the horse in front sent mud splattering on her face. She didn't need to look over her shoulder to see Tom veering off to the left so he could avoid the same fate. She didn't need to look because she heard him laugh.

Slowing down, she saw the carts on the nearby hill had come to a stop. Henrietta appeared to be standing up for a better look.

She must have noticed Evie looking toward the group. Henrietta's arm jutted out and she pointed with jabbing motions.

Following the direction of her hand signal, Evie saw a rider breaking away from the field while the rest of the riders followed the rise and headed for a bridge.

Tom rode up alongside her. "Do you see who it is?"

"It's a woman but I don't recognize her." She might have given up on the chase or grown bored, Evie thought. However, the woman appeared to ride with purpose.

"Which way now? Over or under the bridge?" Tom asked.

She glanced at his pristine white shirt. Rolling her eyes, she said, "I'm already muddy, so let's go under."

They saw the rider disappear behind a copse of trees running alongside the brook, but instead of surging ahead, they slowed down and maintained a discreet distance.

If they were caught, Evie thought it would be easy enough to explain themselves by saying they'd fallen behind and lost the others. Doubling back and following the track leading to the bridge would convince the other rider.

Tom pressed his finger against his lips. Edging forward, Evie thought she saw a flash of white.

Taking care to avoid detection, they moved closer. The rider had definitely stopped.

Evie saw the woman leaning down and whispered, "She's talking to someone." They couldn't get any closer because they'd be seen. Although, she supposed they could pretend they had simply broken away from the field. Which, in fact, they had.

When she suggested it, Tom nodded in agreement.

"I don't suppose the fox is hiding here," he said in a conversational tone meant to be heard.

Evie replied in an equally conversational tone, "Do you realize our species is the only one to hunt and kill for sport?"

"If you disapprove, why did we join in?"

"For the ride, of course. I don't mind that part."

When they came up to the woman, Evie made a show of looking surprised. "Oh, good morning." She thought she recognized her. Although she'd only seen her from a distance, Evie thought she looked like the woman she'd seen talking with Twiggy Lloyd.

The person she'd been talking with tipped his hat and retreated out of sight before they could get a good look at him. At least, they knew it was a man.

Evie had to wonder why the woman's secret rendezvous with another man would be of interest to them. Then she realized, as Lotte Mannering's associate, it would be her job to suspect everyone she encountered and be on the lookout for any suspicious behavior.

"Have you lost your way?" the woman asked.

Evie shook her head. "No, I'm afraid we're not really that enthusiastic about catching the poor old fox or, worse, witnessing his capture."

"You must be from town."

Evie introduced herself and Tom. When the woman introduced herself, Evie smiled. She had been right.

Twiggy Lloyd's wife gave her a whimsical smile. "The Countess of Woodridge? I suppose you haven't embraced country pursuits."

"I'm afraid I have some reservations about some of them. However, I have the good sense to keep my opinions to myself."

"Yes, that's very sensible. I must admit, my heart is never really in it either. I only do it because Twiggy loves it." She looked up toward the trail the others had followed. "I suppose we should at least pretend and rejoin the field. If only for the sake of appearances."

CHAPTER 6

Outfoxed

*A*fter an exuberant gallop across several fields, the master of the hunt decided the fox would live to run free and try to outwit them another day.

"Gone to ground?" Music to her ears, Evie thought. She knew foxhunting had its place in country living. While it served as a leisure sporting activity, it was also deemed a necessity as foxes were perceived as a real threat to livestock.

"Lady Woodridge," Marjorie Devon said as she trotted toward her, her clothes in pristine order. "I hope you enjoyed your ride."

Evie remembered the young woman's earlier greeting had been interrupted by the master of the hunt blowing his horn. Marjorie either wished to pick up where they'd left off and actually engage her in conversation or she had approached her to fulfill her role as a future hostess.

"We did." Evie smiled to herself. When had she started referring to herself as 'we'? And did she mean to include Tom? Yes, she most certainly did.

"Will you be joining us tomorrow?" Marjorie asked.

Evie gave her a sheepish smile. "I'm not sure. I'll have to wait and see how my body responds to today's ride." As Marjorie Devon rode away, Evie exchanged a look with Tom. "I wonder if she just tried to determine my intentions for tomorrow so she could plan her own day. I know she still needs to visit Mrs. Green and I also know she doesn't want me to accompany her."

"And you think she wishes to avoid bumping into you?"

Yes, most definitely, Evie thought. "The question is why." She glanced over at the riders making their way back to the house. Helena Lloyd rode alongside her husband and they appeared to be holding an amiable conversation. Evie imagined her feeling good about something. Had her assignation put her in good spirits?

"I suppose this has been a wild goose chase. We haven't really discovered anything of value," Evie remarked.

"Don't be so hard on yourself. We now know Henrietta and the others are willing to do just about anything to be included."

"True. I take my hat off to them and their ingenuity."

Heading back to the house, they met up with the donkey and cart riding group who waved from a distance and slowed down so Evie and Tom could catch up.

Drawing closer, Evie saw Caro's fingers curled into a tight grip around the side handle. Reading her expression of surprise, Caro exclaimed, "The Dowager almost drove us into a ditch. I never knew a donkey could be pushed to such speeds."

Henrietta leaned in and said, "It's Cousin Henrietta. Remember, we are related." Smiling up at Evie, Henrietta asked, "Did you discover anything interesting about that rider you followed?"

Brushing off some dirt from her face, Evie shared what little she knew.

"Oh, do you think she's having an affair?" Henrietta asked. "How very adventurous to do it right under her husband's nose."

"Something is definitely going on." Although what that might be, Evie had no idea.

"What now?" Toodles asked. "Do we remain here for lunch? I heard someone mention food."

"You can stay, but we're heading back home. I'm sure Lotte has come up with some ideas by now."

"What happened to trying to remain here?" Sara asked.

"I couldn't think of a plan that didn't involve me falling off my horse. I really hope Lotte's had better luck."

"Have a gallop back to the house and see if that will inspire you," Henrietta suggested. Turning to Caro, she said, "Hold tight, Cousin Carolina. We're racing back to Hillsboro Lodge."

Henrietta's donkey must have known better than to baulk at the idea of moving. It took off at surprising speed, its little legs pumping hard and fast, while Sara and Toodles followed close behind in their cart.

"Countess, I think we need to put our heads down. Otherwise, they will beat us back."

"Oh, let them have their fun and little victory."

"Are you sure? You'll have to brace yourself for some serious teasing."

Looking ahead, Evie saw they would have to tackle a couple of fences, hedges and a steep incline while the donkey and carts would have a smooth run of it downhill.

She smiled. "On second thought, giddy up."

Tom rushed after her, warning, "No fences, Countess."

Avoiding the fences meant going the long way around. Knowing he would follow wherever she went, Evie put her head down and made a dash for the nearest hedge.

Evie's breath faltered. At the last minute, she considered pulling on the reins but Poppy had other ideas. She wanted to fly. "Oh, heaven help me."

Tom hollered his warnings even as he matched Evie in tackling the first fence.

As Poppy's front legs lifted and propelled them off the ground, Evie rose slightly off the saddle and leaned in. Instead of keeping her focus on the jump, she found herself distracted by a rider heading off, away from the house. She couldn't be sure, but in that split second, she would have sworn it was Helena Lloyd.

With a yelp, she bounced back and forward as Poppy landed them safely.

Evie glanced over her shoulder in time to see Tom take the jump, his brows furrowed, his mouth set in a grim line.

Before he could recover from the jump, she called out, "Race you to the next fence." Tackling that jump, she then called out, "Race you to the top of the hill."

Several minutes later, they were both out of breath and laughing as they saw Henrietta and the others had actually bested them by beating them back.

"I've just realized we have managed to give ourselves the perfect disguises."

"What disguises?" Tom asked.

"Insouciance, Mr. Winchester. Someone snooping around would have been asking a thousand questions. Instead, we held back and observed."

At least one member of the party had plans they wished to keep secret. They could either discount Helena Lloyd as the person responsible for writing the threatening letters because she had her own personal agenda, that of cheating on her husband, or...

The man she'd met might have been her co-conspirator.

Evie laughed. "I really am becoming quite suspicious of everyone."

"I'm sure it will serve you well in your new endeavor."

The Halton House stable hand, Billy, rushed up to them and held Poppy in place while Evie dismounted. She gave Poppy a pat. "Give her a good feed, Billy. She earned it. You can take the horses back today. I doubt we'll be riding tomorrow."

Caro stood by talking with one of the riders while Henrietta, Sara and Toodles headed toward her.

"I believe we have solved one of your problems," Henrietta declared. "Sterling Wright has just extended an invitation to dinner tonight."

Evie's eyebrows curved up in surprise. "How did you manage that?"

"We decided he's eager to please, so we complimented him on his hospitality."

"Are we all invited?"

"Oh, yes. Absolutely," Henrietta assured her. "His

butler nearly had a fit but he rushed off to make the necessary arrangements."

"Six extra guests. I pity the kitchen staff." While not entirely comfortable with the idea of more or less inviting herself, Evie welcomed the opportunity to observe some of the guests.

A commotion had everyone turning. Twiggy Lloyd stood in the middle of the courtyard hollering his wife's name.

A moment later, someone pointed across the park. Sure enough, Helena Lloyd came trotting across. When she reached her husband, she gave him a bright smile.

Twiggy Lloyd huffed out his displeasure but it didn't seem to affect Helena Lloyd who merely continued to smile.

"Well, what do you make of that?" Henrietta asked.

"They're putting on quite a performance," Sara mused. "Perhaps it's deliberate."

"Are you suggesting they're trying to divert our attention?" Henrietta looked mystified and turned to Evie who merely shrugged.

Without knowing anything about their marital state of affairs, Evie couldn't really say for sure what they were doing or even if their performance had anything to do with Marjorie Devon's threatening letters.

Giving her gloves a tug, she said, "I can't begin to imagine why they would go to such lengths." Turning to Tom, she smiled. "If we're to make it back in time for dinner, we should head back to Halton House now."

Still enthralled by the spectacle, Henrietta waved them off. "Don't worry about us. We'll follow in due course."

Tom laughed under his breath. "Was it only yesterday you had decided to keep them in the dark?"

Settling into the passenger seat, Evie moaned. "Feel free to drive as fast as you can. There is a hot bath with my name on it and I simply can't wait to sink into it."

CHAPTER 7

Halton House

*R*einvigorated by her relaxing bath and with still a few hours to spare, Evie made her way to the library only to be intercepted by Edgar.

"My lady, your cousin is in the drawing room."

"Caro? I mean, Cousin Carolina?"

"No, my lady. Your other cousin."

Overjoyed and somewhat puzzled, Evie asked, "Cousin Ruby?" She was in regular communication with her cousins and not one of them had mentioned making the transatlantic crossing to visit her. *Oh, what a wonderful surprise,* she thought only to then worry she would have to include her in the dinner party.

Edgar shook his head.

Evie took another stab at it. "Cousin Pearl?"

Edgar looked down at his feet.

Evie laughed. "Oh, don't tell me it's Cousin Sapphire."

"Perhaps you should see for yourself, my lady."

They were the only cousins who would think of visiting without an invitation. Evie ran through her entire family tree, but she couldn't really think of any other cousin who'd wish to see her. They were mostly male and too busy to pay her any attention.

Edgar turned and led the way to the drawing room. When he reached the door, he stepped aside to let Evie through.

Walking in, Evie's gaze went to the first person she saw. Caro sat on the edge of a sofa with her hands clasped and looking somewhat tense. As Evie took another step inside the room, Caro turned.

"Oh, heavens. At last," her maid exclaimed.

Evie's gaze jumped from Caro to the person sitting opposite her. Presumably, her cousin.

"Hello." Evie searched the woman's face for any family resemblance but found none.

Could she be a distant cousin she'd never met or even heard of?

She struck quite a dramatic pose with her legs crossed and her foot, clad in a velvet shoe embroidered with what looked like a Chinese symbol, swaying from side to side. As she studied Evie, she adjusted a monocle eyeglass on her eye.

Evie stood looking at her and feeling quite entranced by the eyepiece. She'd seen a few of them but mostly in display cases as, these days, anyone needing to correct their eyesight wore spectacles.

Caro bounced slightly on her seat as if belatedly

remembering to be excited. "Look, Cousin Evie. It's Cousin... Ophelia."

The effort to hold the black rimmed monocle in place meant Cousin Ophelia's eye looked smaller while the other eye looked larger. Also, she had her cheek lifted slightly to help keep the eyepiece in place. That gave her a lopsided smile.

Cousin Ophelia chortled. "Cousin Evie is lost for words. Our last encounter ended in an argument over something silly. I'd hoped you'd put it all behind you." Cousin Ophelia's lopsided smile grew. She sat back and adjusted a cigarette onto an elegant holder. Lighting it, she held it against her lips but did not draw on it. Evie watched a curl of smoke dance around her and waft away.

"Cousin Ophelia?" Evie looked over her shoulder.

Edgar stood by the door looking up at the ceiling.

Evie knew she could say anything in front of him and he would not repeat it to a single, living soul.

Looking back at Cousin Ophelia, Evie asked, "Is this what you came up with?"

Lotte Mannering shrugged. "I had you fooled for a moment."

Admittedly, she hadn't recognized Lotte at first. The effort it took to keep the monocle in place distorted her features to the point that Lotte really became unrecognizable.

As for her clothes...

She had dressed as a Bohemian in a striking coat with red and white stripes and a floppy black velvet beret on her head.

"We were just discussing tonight's dinner," Caro said.

"Oh, I see. Am I to turn up at Sterling Wright's house with an extra guest?"

Lotte smiled. "I'm sure you'll have no trouble arranging it, Cousin Evie."

Sighing, Evie sat down opposite her new cousin. "Please tell me you're the black sheep of the family and no one ever talks about you. You've been turned away from everyone's house and, here you are, taking refuge at Halton House."

"That sounds like a solid background story but here's something else I've come up with. I've spent several years wandering around the Far East and India. There are many months I cannot account for and my correspondence has been vague so you can't really help to fill in the gaps."

Evie checked the clock on the mantle. "I suppose the vagueness will lend credibility." Looking at Edgar, she asked, "Where's Mr. Winchester?"

She heard a stifled laugh which seemed to come from a corner chair turned away from the room. As the laughter grew, Tom showed himself.

"My apologies, Countess. Before you ask, I didn't hide on purpose. These two simply caught me in the act of napping."

"Well, now that we have all that sorted out, have you come up with a new plan? Something other than dressing up as my notorious cousin."

Just as Lotte was about to respond, a footman approached Edgar and whispered in his ear.

Edgar cleared his throat. "There is a telephone call for Caro."

Her lady's maid and occasional cousin, thrice removed, surged to her feet and excused herself.

A moment later, she returned. "That was Mrs. Green calling to alert us of Miss Marjorie Devon's imminent arrival at her establishment."

"Really? And why on earth is Mrs. Green informing us?"

Caro sat down. "When we returned from the hunt, the Dowager, or rather, Cousin Henrietta... decided she would stop in the village and drop in on Mrs. Green. We all accompanied her and one thing led to another and Mrs. Green agreed to keep us informed."

Tom smiled at Evie. "All this happened while you were having a leisurely soak in the tub. You should do it more often."

"I see. So we have now engaged the services of Mrs. Green."

Caro nodded. "Apparently, Cousin Henrietta's butler has several spies in the village but, Cousin Henrietta assures us, none from Halton House. Anyway, she thought this new investigation required some fresh recruits. Hence her appeal to Mrs. Green."

Evie sat back and stared at Lotte. "I believe you have sought out the wrong Woodridge to partner up with. Henrietta has proven herself to be quite resourceful."

Lotte grinned. "There's always room for expansion and inclusion."

Evie rubbed her finger along her temple. "Just so we're on the same page, which side of the family do you belong to?"

"Your husband's side but, like Cousin Carolina, I am several times removed and have even been ostracized and banished. To this day, there are still some Woodridge family members who refuse to acknowledge me." Lotte leaned forward. "In fact, if you consult the family Bible, you will find my name has been struck off so effectively, there isn't even a single trace of it."

"And how exactly did you find your way into our good graces again?"

Lotte smiled. "Bygones. That's your motto."

"Cousin Evie," Caro shifted to the edge of her seat. "Shouldn't you start making your way to Mrs. Green's establishment?"

Evie's gaze automatically sought out Tom. Yes, she was now taking directions from her maid.

"Of course. Thank you for reminding me. Tom, shall we go?"

Caro, who had no trouble slipping in and out of character, rushed to the door, saying, "I'll fetch your hat and coat, milady."

Moments later, as she waited in the hall, Evie paced around.

Tom stood by, entertained by the sight. "Something tells me you're not amused."

Evie swung around. "I'm trying to work out how I'm going to explain an extra guest to Sterling Wright. At this rate, I'll be known as the Countess who blithely imposes on everyone's generosity. A moocher. A sponger, going around loading up on free food and entertainment. A freeloader. Is there such a word? If there isn't, it should be included in our vocabulary. Yes, that sounds just about right, the freeloading Countess."

Tom laughed. "Sterling Wright is keen to have you as his guest. He already said you were a positive influence on his fiancée. I doubt he'll mind if you bring along another guest."

Evie gave him a worried look. "I've never seen anyone arrive at an invitation only event with an entourage of extra guests. Mark my word, this will be talked about."

Caro rushed down the stairs and helped Evie into the coat.

"Thank you, Caro." As she turned to leave, she said, "Feel free to rummage through my wardrobe. Cousin Carolina will need something suitable to wear to tonight's dinner."

Lifting her collar up, she led the way to the roadster.

As Tom settled in, he said, "Aren't you concerned your lady's maid will get ideas and start looking to improve her situation in life?"

Evie laughed. "Caro is irreplaceable but if she wishes to move on, then I'll have to grin and bear it. However, I think she's having too much fun to ever consider leaving."

Caro rushed out of the house. "I thought you might need a blanket. It's quite chilly out here, milady."

They drove the short distance in silence, both Tom and Evie smiling at some private thought.

When they reached the village, Evie suggested, "You should leave the roadster somewhere out of sight. I don't want to spook Marjorie Devon."

They saw only a couple of people out and about. Entering Mrs. Green's dressmaking establishment, Evie removed her gloves and walked to the fireplace to warm her hands. When no one came to greet them, she assumed Mrs. Green was busy with Miss Devon in one of the private parlors.

Tom joined her by the fireplace, sitting down in a comfortable winged armchair.

"The more I think about it," Evie whispered, "the more

I like Lotte's disguise. She'll now be able to wander around at leisure. As my cousin, no one will suspect her of following Marjorie Devon around the place. She might even be able to befriend Marjorie Devon."

Hearing footsteps approaching, Evie fell silent.

Mrs. Green appeared around a corner. "Lady Woodridge. I hope I haven't kept you waiting." She looked over her shoulder and lowered her voice. "I'm afraid it's been a wasted trip. Miss Devon left only a few minutes ago. She came in for a fitting and was supposed to wait until my seamstress could make a quick alteration but she hurried off. She's asked me to have the gown delivered to Hillsboro Lodge. So I'm afraid she won't be returning."

Well, so much for shadowing her every step. "Did she say why she couldn't wait for the alterations?"

Mrs. Green made an open-hand gesture. "I left her in the parlor and when I returned she was already out the door."

"Thank you, Mrs. Green."

"Is there anything else I can assist you with, my lady?"

Evie looked around. "Actually, may I step inside the parlor?"

"Would you like me to bring you a selection of fabrics to peruse?"

"Oh, no. I… I just need a moment to think." Seeing her downcast expression, Evie changed her mind. "Actually, yes. That would be a wonderful idea. I need a new evening dress." Mrs. Green brightened, but only slightly. Evie realized only a few people would see her in an evening dress. However, something more practical she could wear out and about might be seen by more people. "Oh, and a coat. Yes, I definitely need a new coat."

This time, Mrs. Green smiled. "I have the loveliest fabric, my lady. I'm sure you will love it. I won't be long."

Evie slipped into the small parlor fitted out for special clients and looked around. There was a velvet chaise in the corner and a matching chair near the fireplace with a small table and lamp next to it.

Evie walked around the small space and then sat down. Tapping her foot, she tried to picture Marjorie Devon coming in earlier. Why had she left so quickly?

A fire had been prepared so she could not have found the room uncomfortable. She sat back and drummed her fingers on the armrest.

A stack of paper sat on the small table. Evie looked away only to lean in for a closer look. She couldn't remember ever seeing writing paper in the room. Mrs. Green carried a small leather-bound book she used to take down measurements, so she had no need for more paper.

Picking up the sheet on top, she studied it. She could just make out the slightest indentation showing a couple of words.

Inspiration struck. Setting the paper down, she went to stand by the fireplace and, leaning down, she ran her fingertip along the edge. It came away with a layer of soot which she used to brush along the piece of paper. As she did, two words were revealed.

"Rosebud Green," she read. Just then, Mrs. Green came in carrying a selection of fabrics.

Evie made quick work of folding the piece of paper and slipping it inside her pocket.

"Oh, these are lovely. I believe you already have my

measurements. Do you think you could start working on a coat for me, please?"

"Yes, certainly, my lady. Straightaway. What about the evening gown?"

"Oh, I'll have to think about that one. My maid is very particular about the colors I wear." She gave her a brisk smile. "By the way, is there such a color as rosebud green?"

Mrs. Green thought about it for a moment. "It could be a new color but not one I'm aware of."

"So you haven't heard it mentioned recently?"

"No, I can't say that I have, my lady."

What could it mean and had Marjorie Devon written it?

Walking out of the parlor, Evie imagined Marjorie sitting down and suddenly remembering something. She then pictured the young woman writing it down, putting the piece of paper away and rushing out because…

Because rosebud green had reminded her of something important she needed to do?

"That was quick," Tom said and rose to his feet. "Where to now?"

"Back to Halton House. Heaven knows how many more family members will be waiting for me." Inspiration struck again. Evie turned and smiled at Mrs. Green. "Do you happen to remember what Miss Devon wore this afternoon?"

CHAPTER 8

Dinner is served

Hillsboro Lodge

$\mathcal{L}$otte congratulated Evie on her ingenuity. They had spent some time studying the piece of paper and trying to decipher its meaning right along with Marjorie Devon's curious behavior.

There had to be a reason for the threatening letters. If they could keep a close eye on her, they might get to the bottom of it all.

Looking up and across the dining table, Evie lifted her wine glass, both to take a sip and to toast Lotte's transformation into her Cousin Ophelia.

She wore a stylish suit in black satin with wide legged

trousers and a glittering scarf studded with beads that glimmered like the crystals on the chandelier above. Instead of a headband, she wore a silver satin turban with a black feather. As it turned out, Lotte traveled with a set of disguises for any occasion.

After an afternoon of practicing, she had mastered the art of holding her monocle in place. However, after the second glass of wine, Evie could see it risked falling into the soup.

Lotte, or rather, Cousin Ophelia, tipped her head back and produced a loud roar of a laugh at something Twiggy Lloyd said.

While Twiggy Lloyd's remark had amused Lotte, Marjorie Devon, who sat next to Twiggy Lloyd, did not look amused.

If Sterling Wright had recognized Lotte he did not let on. He sat next to Evie and his remark set her at ease.

"I'm glad to see your cousin is enjoying herself."

"You sound surprised," Evie replied.

"To tell the truth, I did not expect to experience the pleasure of such lively company in the country. In fact, I'd almost given up hope of enjoying the type of entertainment one is used to in town. In the country, everyone appears eager to keep up appearances and behave in an acceptable manner. Don't get me wrong, I don't expect to see anyone dancing on top of tables."

Cousin Ophelia laughed again giving Evie the opportunity to study Sterling Wright. He really didn't appear to have noticed the disguise.

It reminded her of an incident she'd read about when she'd first arrived in England in 1910 about a hoax masterminded by the prankster *Horace de Vere Cole*.

A group of friends had disguised themselves as Abyssinian royalty and had sent a telegram to the Commander of the Home Fleet saying the group of Abyssinians were due to arrive in Dorset and he should arrange to meet them. Regardless of the short notice, they were greeted with pomp and ceremony, with a band playing the British and Abyssinian national anthems. Absolutely no one had suspected a hoax until the prankster leaked the story to the newspapers.

People see what they expect to see, Evie mused as Cousin Ophelia shared a tale about a ride on an elephant in India, which further embellished her disguise.

Evie turned her attention to Marjorie Devon who sat across the table from her.

They hadn't discussed tactics so Evie decided to focus on observing and keeping her eyes open for anything unusual. So far, she hadn't heard anyone mention *rosebud green*. But she had come to believe that could be a key to the threats.

"I hope your cousin attends the ball," Sterling said.

"She wouldn't miss it for the world. Thank you for extending the invitation."

Cousin Ophelia gestured to a footman who promptly refilled her glass and not for the first time. She'd already imbibed a couple of drinks before dinner. Maybe they would witness some dancing on tables, after all.

"I feel for your grandmama," Sterling said. "Lady Henrietta is trying without success to get a conversation out of Matthew Prentiss but I'm afraid the man only ever talks about horses and money."

"Does he bemoan the lack of it?" Evie asked.

"Oh, no. He's a banker and that's all he knows. Apart

from horses, of course. He's been trying to induce me to partner with him in the purchase of a horse. At least, that's all he's been talking to me about but, in reality, I know he wishes to invest in my latest acquisition, Mighty Warrior." He picked up his glass of wine and looked at it. "I'm thinking of changing its name to something quaint."

"Rosebud green," Evie suggested and watched to see his reaction.

"That's interesting. Where have I heard it before? I suppose it will come to me."

"Have you asked your fiancée for suggestions?"

"I did. She liked Bonbon."

"That's sweet."

He nodded. "Marjorie is partial to chocolates."

Could rosebud green be the name of a confectionary? "What color is the horse?"

"Brown."

Just brown? How unusual. Normally, owners would note the remarkable markings and praise the unique shade of color.

"It's arriving tomorrow. I'm hoping to come up with a new name before his previous owner, George Stevens, arrives."

"Is he attending the ball?"

"Yes and I think he's had a change of heart and wishes to strike a deal."

"Seller's remorse?"

"Something like that. One never likes to ask but I believe he might have experienced financial difficulties which he has now overcome."

"And you want to change the name of the horse to affirm your ownership."

He grinned. "I'm hoping he'll get the message. I'd hate to have to spell it out to him."

Evie thought she heard him murmur *rosebud green* a couple of times as if still trying to recall where he'd heard it before.

Was *rosebud green* nothing more than a sudden stroke of inspiration? Maybe the word combination had come to Marjorie and she'd rushed home to suggest it to her fiancé. Maybe that's why he thought he'd heard it mentioned.

With the last course served and enjoyed, it was Evie's duty, as the highest-ranking member of the party, to rise. The ladies followed suit and made their way out of the dining room leaving the gentlemen to their brandy and cigars. Cousin Ophelia swayed several times but succeeded in straightening herself, twice by holding on to Evie.

"Did you plan that?" Evie whispered. She knew Lotte could hold her liquor but she'd never seen her drinking so much.

She glanced at her inebriated soon to be business partner in time to see her wink.

Whatever plan she'd hatched clearly involved drinking herself into a stupor or somehow pretending to do so.

When they settled in the drawing room, Lotte helped herself to a glass of brandy and tossed it back in one gulp.

"Don't be surprised if I fall asleep in a chair," she slurred.

"We'll have to carry you out to the motor car."

Lotte winked at her again. "Or, you could just leave me here to sleep it off."

Joining them, Tom said, "Do you need propping up?"

Clearly, he'd noticed Lotte's excessive drinking.

"I think this is her plan," Evie whispered and pictured Lotte haunting the hallways in the middle of the night. What did she hope to find? She wished they could all just stop and decide how they were going to proceed. "What are you doing here? You're supposed to be drinking your brandy and smoking your cigar with the men."

Tom winced. "I'm not really a brandy drinker or a cigar smoker."

"That's beside the point. You should be there listening to their conversation."

"Why? Do you think one of them is going to talk about *rosebud green*?"

"Maybe."

Caro joined them. "There were not enough gentlemen so I sat between Miss Devon and Cousin Henrietta. She spent the entire dinner poking me in the ribs and prompting me to ask Miss Devon pertinent questions."

"And did you?" Evie asked.

Caro shrugged. "I couldn't think of anything that might lead her to divulge the secrets of *rosebud green*." Caro winced. "I really don't respond well to violent prompts. I wouldn't be surprised if I wake up with bruises on my side."

Lowering her voice to a whisper, Evie said, "I wish we could dismiss it but when I mentioned rosebud green to Sterling Wright he said it sounded familiar."

Henrietta and Sara entered the drawing room with Marjorie Devon between them.

The young woman looked somewhat bewildered. She searched the room and, finding Helena Lloyd helping herself to a drink, she excused herself and walked across the room to join her.

"What on earth were you saying to Marjorie?" Evie asked. "She looked almost desperate to escape you."

Henrietta laughed. "We were simply telling her about the joys of country living. The poor girl has no idea."

"I think you've just succeeded in frightening her away. Sterling Wright is going to be mystified when she suddenly packs her bags and demands to return to London. How did you phrase your information?"

"Politely, of course. We told her she'd have to entertain the local vicar. The poor man stutters. But I fail to see why that should put her off. Oh, I also mentioned the vicar enjoys rosebuds, especially the ones tinged with green. That's when she excused herself."

Had that been coincidental or had Marjorie Devon reacted to Henrietta's mention of words that had also made her suddenly leave Mrs. Green's establishment?

Henrietta glanced at Lotte. "Why is Cousin Ophelia tilting?"

"Never mind her. I've just remembered something. With all the excitement about the piece of paper and rosebud green, I forgot to mention something else. We need to know where Marjorie Devon went after she left Mrs. Green's establishment in such a hurry. Can you engage your secret service people? Someone must have seen where she went."

"I'll alert my butler as soon as we return. He'll be only too happy to help, I'm sure."

Evie's heart gave a thump of alarm.

"Countess? You look pale."

"Where's Toodles?"

As if on cue, her granny walked in and made her way to the drinks table.

"Were you afraid something had happened to her?" Tom asked.

She didn't want to admit it. However, she couldn't help feeling on edge. "I can't explain it. Lotte's investigation has been almost uneventful. Now, I feel something is about to happen."

"Either you have developed a nose for such things or you're disappointed with your official foray into the world of private detecting and you actually *want* something to happen."

"What nonsense. I hope you're not about to label me the doomsayer Countess."

Tom laughed. "Oh, there's an idea."

"What did I miss?" Toodles asked as she approached them.

"Your granddaughter thought you might have become a victim. Have you been generous with her in your will?" Tom asked.

Rolling her eyes, Evie smiled at Toodles. "It seems Cousin Ophelia has overdone it. She's fallen asleep and we might have to impose on Sterling Wright's generosity." For effect, Evie nudged Cousin Ophelia with her foot and, raising her voice slightly, she added, "See, she's quite out of it and almost a deadweight, I'm sure. We won't be able to budge her or even stir her awake."

CHAPTER 9

The sleep of the innocent

Halton House

"*I* slept like a log," Toodles declared as she sat down to breakfast the next morning.

"Well, I'm glad someone did." Evie looked over at the clock on the mantle. At some point, she would have to send someone over to Hillsboro Lodge to deliver a change of clothes for Cousin Ophelia. Only then would she know Lotte had come to no harm during the night.

Toodles looked up from her hearty breakfast. "Oh? Did your conscience keep you awake?"

It took a moment for Evie to remember the remark

Tom had made in jest the previous evening. "Grans, I promise I'm not after your fortune."

"And yet that doesn't inspire confidence in me. Perhaps you should add something about not wishing me harm." Toodles took a sip of her coffee. "Actually, I think you'll have to be more specific because you could kill me and declare you never actually *wished* to kill me…"

Tom entered the morning room and helped himself to a generous breakfast. "I seem to have walked in on a private conversation."

Evie looked at Edgar who stood by overseeing the footmen. "Edgar, could you please send word to Caro. Tell her we're expecting Lady Carolina to breakfast with us."

Edgar inclined his head and, bless his soul, proceeded to do as asked without a single word of disapproval.

Turning to Tom, Evie smiled. "Thanks to you, my grandmother is going to be locking her doors and looking over her shoulder." She glanced at Toodles. "I'd watch out for this one. Maybe he wants to get in your good graces and inherit from you."

Edgar returned momentarily and informed Evie, "I found Caro in the kitchen. She was surprised by your request but she assured me she will rush to prepare Lady Carolina."

"Thank you, Edgar."

Toodles took a leisurely sip of her coffee. "A part of me thinks I should find that conversation disturbing, but I read the newspapers this morning and I must say I prefer this reality to the one out there."

Evie turned to the butler again, "Oh, Edgar."

Edgar stopped and turned. "Yes, my lady?"

"Before Caro attends to Lady Carolina, ask her to

please collect some suitable clothes for Cousin Ophelia. As soon as they're ready, Edmonds can drive over to Hillsboro Lodge and deliver them."

"Certainly, my lady."

Frowning, Evie looked at Toodles. Belatedly, she said, "Why would you find that conversation disturbing?"

Toodles shrugged. "You're right. I have no reason to do so. I only hope Caro doesn't suffer some sort of personality disorder. You should at least give the girl some warning."

"Thank you for your concern, Grans. But you shouldn't underestimate Caro. She is most efficient and quick to jump into action."

"And are we jumping into action today?" Tom asked.

Evie couldn't think of what else they could do. "The Hunt Ball is tonight. Going to Hillsboro Lodge this morning or this afternoon is out of the question. Even if I could come up with a reasonable excuse to make a sudden appearance before tonight." So far, no one had been hurt. However, Evie wouldn't mind discovering the identity of the person who'd sent the threatening letters. What if they meant to take their threats a step further?

"We could spy from afar," Toodles suggested.

Evie looked up at the ceiling. "Why is my mind suddenly flooded with images of you climbing up a tree and me following you?"

"Where does that leave me?" Tom asked.

Evie grinned. "Being a gentleman and making sure we don't fall."

As they turned their focus to their breakfast, Edgar returned and, soon after, they heard hurried steps approaching. The door opened and Henrietta walked in, her hand to her chest.

Henrietta glanced around the room. "Oh, thank goodness. You are all still here."

Sara appeared behind Henrietta. "I told you we didn't need to hurry. No one in their right mind sets out at this time of the morning."

"Have you had breakfast?" Evie asked even as Edgar directed the footmen to organize two extra place settings.

"No. I skipped breakfast because I have news I received early this morning," Henrietta declared. "News from you know who and it couldn't wait."

News relating to Miss Devon's activities? It had to be and, clearly, Henrietta wished to protect her informant's identity which happened to be her butler.

Henrietta began by saying, "Yesterday afternoon, Miss Marjorie Devon departed Mrs. Green's establishment in haste. Of course, we all knew that," Henrietta gave a firm nod. "But here's what we didn't know. The baker's wife claims she might have been injured if she hadn't stopped and turned to shout at her husband. You see, she had just been about to cross the road when Miss Devon's motor sped by at full speed. The baker's store, as you know, is located at the end of the street so the baker's wife can confirm Miss Devon left the village without stopping."

"But what about before that?" Sara asked. "I've been trying to reason with Henrietta but she feels this is enough to prove Miss Devon did not stop elsewhere. I disagree."

Henrietta smiled. "You were so fierce in your opposition, I withheld the rest of the information."

Before Henrietta and Sara could tangle themselves up

in an argument, Evie prodded Henrietta to divulge the rest of her closely guarded secret.

"Miss Devon did make another stop. She went to the tearoom. She only spent a few minutes in there and when she exited she carried a small parcel."

Sara harrumphed. "A small parcel? She probably purchased some cakes and that's why the baker's wife is so intent on portraying her exodus from the village with such dark undertones."

Henrietta tilted her head. "Sara, I never knew you could be so melodramatic." After a moment, she added, "But I suppose you're right. I will have to check with my sources to see if there is any animosity between the baker's wife and the tearoom owner. As it is, the fact Miss Devon stopped to purchase some cakes tells us that we might have been hasty in assuming she fled from the dressmaker's establishment after scribbling a cryptic message." Henrietta drummed her fingers on the table and said in a pensive tone, "*Rosebud green*. What could it possibly mean?"

Everyone sat back and murmured, "*Rosebud green*."

When Caro, dressed as Lady Carolina, walked in, she found them still staring into space. "Heavens, have you all been hypnotized?"

Evie snapped out of her reverie. "Cousin Carolina. Good morning." In a moment of clarity, she remembered she was also talking to Caro, her maid, who had already enjoyed her breakfast with the rest of the servants. Suddenly, she couldn't resist the temptation. "We're still eating breakfast. Do join us. You must be famished."

Caro patted her stomach. "Oh, actually..."

Henrietta encouraged. "Oh, don't be shy. We know you have a healthy appetite."

Caro relented. "Perhaps some tea and toast."

Henrietta smiled at Caro and gave her a brief summary. "We were just discussing the news I brought."

"I must say," Evie mused, "I had hoped Miss Devon had rushed to the postal office to send a telegram."

Henrietta looked at her with interest. "In order to alert someone? Did you think *rosebud green* was some sort of code name?"

"It could be a destination," Caro offered as she buttered her toast.

They all turned to look at her.

Evie clapped and exclaimed, "Cousin Carolina, that is ingenious."

Her maid's cheeks flooded with a twinge of pink. "It's something worth considering. It could also be the name of a horse. People place bets on them and maybe… maybe she received a tip or inside information and only then, when she sat at Mrs. Green's, did she remember it."

Sara smiled. "I've heard say breakfast is the most important meal of the day because it fuels your brain." She surged to her feet and headed straight for the sideboard with its abundant offer of food.

Taking a sip of her tea, Caro said, "I suppose we'll be hearing from Cousin Ophelia soon. I… I mean, Caro told me you asked her to prepare some clothes for her. I'm guessing she survived the night."

Evie looked at Caro for a moment and wondered if Toodles had been right in expressing concern for her. She hoped playing the dual roles didn't become too confusing in her mind.

"If something happened to her, Sterling Wright would have informed us." Evie turned to Edgar who lifted an eyebrow.

"With all due respect, my lady, if I had heard any news, I would have conveyed the information to you without delay."

"Yes, of course. I have no doubt you would do so."

The door opened and they all turned only to be disappointed when a footman entered carrying a fresh pot of coffee.

"Lotte told me being a private detective requires a great deal of patience because a lot of the time is spent simply waiting for something to happen."

"In this case," Henrietta said, "We are waiting for something to happen to Miss Devon. Since she is being threatened, we have to assume the threats are real. I find that rather morbid."

"Does that mean we also have to assume she will not abide by whatever she's been asked to do in order to be free of repercussions?" Sara asked.

Evie brightened. Of course, the threats had to be related to something. Had Marjorie been asked to do something and had she ignored the request?

"That's just it," Evie mused, "we can't know for sure if she's received demands. I think we have to assume someone is simply out to make her pay for some sort of transgression. There are numerous threatening letters but Lotte only read one of them."

Toodles set her cup down. "Why would Sterling Wright engage Lotte's services and then withhold vital information that might help her solve the case?"

"That's a very good point, Grans. But he only hired Lotte to follow his fiancée."

Henrietta shuddered. "The mystery deepens."

"Or perhaps we're reading too much into it," Caro suggested. "Last night, I observed Sterling Wright and I came away thinking he struck me as being somewhat oblivious. You know, the type of person who thinks if you ignore something it will go away."

Evie shook her head. "I'm not so sure I agree. He did, after all, engage Lotte's services."

"Yes, but he diminished her ability to do her job by not giving her access to the full picture," Caro reasoned.

Evie happened to catch Tom looking at her. When he raised his eyebrows, she assumed he thought Caro had made a valid point.

Sara disagreed. "He's a man and they don't always know what's best. Lotte should have pushed for more information."

At that point, Evie realized her venture into the world of private detecting would really become a family affair. Had they set out to make themselves useful on purpose?

She glanced at the clock again and groaned under her breath.

Annoyingly, she didn't know enough about Lotte Mannering's personal traits. For all she knew, the lady detective enjoyed sleeping in and they could be waiting all morning for her to make an appearance.

"I think I'll go out for a walk to clear my head."

"I'll join you," Tom said.

"Yes, a walk sounds like a very good idea." Henrietta stood up and nudged Sara.

"Oh, yes. A blast of cold is just the thing to shock the body into responding."

They all turned to Caro and Toodles.

Toodles lifted her cup of coffee. "We'll be right along as soon as we finish our breakfast."

Evie walked out into the hall and realized she could not call on Caro to fetch her coat. "I suppose I can fend for myself," she mused as she made her way upstairs.

In her room, she selected a coat but had trouble finding her gloves and a scarf. After searching through all the drawers, she finally had what she needed so she made her way down only to find Caro overtaking her and rushing down the stairs. To her surprise, she had changed into her maid's outfit again.

"Cousin Carolina," Evie exclaimed.

"No, milady, it's Caro."

Evie's mind spun for a moment. Why had Cousin Carolina changed back to Caro? "I thought you were coming for a walk with us."

Caro didn't stop. Continuing down the stairs, she looked over her shoulder at Evie and said, "I can't stop now, milady. Must rush off."

"B-but why? Where are you going?" Evie found herself hurrying down the stairs after her. When she reached the bottom of the stairs, she found the others all huddled around Caro who gave a firm nod and then rushed out the door.

"Would someone please tell me what's going on?" Heavens, she'd only been upstairs for a few minutes...

What could possibly have happened during her brief absence?

Henrietta stepped forward. "Mrs. Green just telephoned to say she has been asked to personally deliver a gown to Hillsboro Lodge. Sara had the bright idea of suggesting Caro go along as her assistant."

"But what if Miss Devon recognizes her?" Evie asked.

"What nonsense. Miss Devon is not going to notice Caro. Women like her never pay any attention to servants."

Evie glanced at Tom. When he shrugged, she knew he hadn't even tried to talk them out of it.

"And how will she get there? Edmonds has already left, I'm sure he has."

"Mrs. Green has organized transportation," Tom said.

"Evangeline, I hope you don't feel we have undermined your authority as a newly fledged lady detective."

"Oh, heavens… Of course not…"

Henrietta continued, "We considered waiting for you."

"Oh, I… I couldn't find my gloves."

Henrietta gave her a whimsical smile.

Evie looked heavenwards. If she had trouble finding her gloves, what hope did she have of getting to the bottom of a mystery?

CHAPTER 10

The waiting game

The drawing room
Halton House

*E*vie tried to use the time to catch her breath. With two people out there doing who knew what, they had unanimously decided to cancel their walk. Evie paced around the drawing room and kept glancing at the clock.

It had been an hour since her maid, Caro, had left to join Mrs. Green to deliver Miss Devon's dress.

"How long does it take to try on a dress?" Evie fumed. "And where is Lotte?"

The edge of Sara's lip lifted. "You mean, Cousin Ophelia."

"Thank you for trying to humor me. I'm beginning to think I'm not cut out for this line of work. And… Where is Edmonds? He should have returned by now if not with Lotte in tow, then with news about her wellbeing." Turning, she looked at Edgar only to realize he had made himself present all morning. Usually, if she wanted something, she had to ring for him.

"I'm sorry, my lady. He has yet to return. Would you like me to send someone to Hillsboro Lodge?"

"Oh, heavens, no. We can't afford to lose any more people."

Henrietta laughed. "Evangeline, you are being very sensible to keep your troops in place. I fear you may be right in thinking we cannot afford any more casualties."

Rather than be annoyed by the remark, Evie took a bow. "I'm glad you're amused, Henrietta. I can't help fretting."

Sara said, her voice filled with understanding, "Only because you are worried you might disrupt Lotte's investigation. I believe you are suffering from a bout of fear of failure. Don't be discouraged by a lack of news. It will come soon enough and then…" Sara smiled, "you will mobilize your troops."

"Meanwhile, we could play a game of cards," Henrietta suggested. "Any discussion involving Miss Devon will only lead you to become more frustrated."

Evie stopped pacing and swung toward the door. "Actually, there is something useful I could do." She headed toward the library and, not surprisingly, the others followed.

Evie perused the shelves until she found what she wanted. "There are several road maps. If we all take one, we might be lucky and come across *rosebud green* somewhere."

Tom eventually walked in, his hands in his pockets. "What are we doing?"

"We're looking for *rosebud green*. Caro suggested it might be a place. And, the more I think about it, the more I believe she is right."

"Could it be a village green?" he asked.

Evie looked up from her road map. "Yes! Yes, it could be and I hope it isn't because those don't seem to be listed in these maps."

Henrietta nodded. "I am reminded of Newington Green in north London. My nanny lived there after she retired and I visited her once. She had a great interest in history and I remember her telling me the area had once been a wilderness and Henry VIII had used a house on the south side of the green as a base for hunting wild boars and such that roamed the forest. I realize that information is of no use to us. Although, if we ask around, someone might recognize the name as a real place."

Ask around? Where? Evie frowned at her. "That would require leaving the house and, as you said, I don't want to lose any more people."

Picking up one of the maps, Tom settled down on a chair by the fireplace. "England suddenly looks very big."

"Perhaps we should narrow our search," Sara suggested. "And then spread out."

"And where do you suggest we begin?" Henrietta asked.

"We could start near Hillsboro Lodge and follow our

way back to town. Do we know how Miss Devon made her way from London?"

"Most likely by train," Evie said. "She might have seen a sign that read *rosebud green* on her way here."

Edgar cleared his throat. When Evie looked up, he said, "I have just spotted Edmonds driving up, my lady."

Everyone set their road maps down and surged to their feet.

"At last," Henrietta exclaimed. "I hope Lotte is with him and knows all about *rosebud green*. The prospect of combing through road maps is making me squint and I don't need extra lines around my eyes. Also, I am of a certain age and I could expire at any moment. *Rosebud green* would be the last words I utter."

Piling out of the library, they headed toward the entrance to Halton House and stepped out, their arms crossed against the cold wind whipping about.

To their relief, they saw Lotte jump out of the Duesenberg, laughing at something she said to Edmonds.

When she spotted the welcoming party, Lotte adjusted her monocle, tipped her head back, and laughed again.

"She's still in character," Henrietta mused. "I think I'd like to try playing the role of someone else. I'm sure it would feel quite liberating and as refreshing as going on a trip."

"Maybe we should all try it," Sara said. "Since Evie is going to become involved in investigations and we are clearly going to lend our assistance, we should be prepared for the prospect of disguising ourselves."

When Lotte reached them, they all talked at once.

"We were so worried about you," Evie said.

"Yes, Evangeline's footprints are quite visible on the carpet. Do tell us what you discovered."

Toodles, who had finally joined them, asked, "Did you get caught?"

"*Rosebud green*. Does that ring a bell?" Sara asked.

Still laughing, Lotte looked at Tom. "I see Tom can't get a word in edgewise."

Continuing to talk all at once, they all urged her to come in out of the cold.

"What on earth took you so long?" Evie asked as Edgar helped Lotte out of her coat.

"If you recall, I enjoyed quite a few glasses of wine last night."

"Are you going to tell me you spent the night and this morning sleeping it off?"

"I spent part of the morning catching up on the sleep I missed out on last night when I roamed the hallways of Hillsboro Lodge."

"So while everyone slept, you lurked about? Looking for what?" Henrietta asked. A second later, she put her hand to her chest. "Good heavens, did you press your ear to people's doors?"

Lotte merely smiled. "A good detective never reveals her trade secrets." Looking at Evie, she added, "Except to you, in due course."

"And us, as well," Sara demanded. "We have been quite helpful."

Walking up to the fireplace in the hall, Lotte stretched her hands out to warm them. "What's this about rosebud green?"

"Clearly nothing of importance since you don't know about it. Tell us what you discovered," Henrietta urged.

"Well… soon after you left, everyone had a nightcap. The conversation revolved around horses and the new racing season coming up. Pamela Prentiss excused herself saying she had a headache. While Marjorie Devon and Helena Lloyd sat without saying a word. I had the impression they were both deep in thought. When I glimpsed the first person make a move to retire for the evening, I made a point of stirring awake with a loud snort."

"How peculiar," Sara observed.

"Not necessarily. I wanted them to notice me. A polite yawn would not have achieved the desired result."

"Make the sound for us," Henrietta invited. "I wish to hear it."

Lotte complied by tilting her head back, lolling it from side to side and then emitting a loud, garbled snort which had an impressive undertone of surprise. Henrietta said as much.

Lotte smiled. "Thank you for noticing. That is precisely the effect I aimed for. Anyhow, saying it was too late in the evening to stir the chauffeur awake, Sterling Wright offered to put me up for the night and summoned a couple of footmen to assist me up the stairs. I remained in character by becoming a deadweight even as I sang a drunken ditty. I feel rather guilty because I believe one footman is currently nursing a sore back."

"Astonishing," Sara declared. "I wish I'd been there to witness it."

Lotte looked up as if trying to organize her thoughts. "Oh, there was mention of a guest arriving today. I noticed Marjorie shifting in her seat and glancing at Helena Lloyd. Her eyes widened ever so slightly."

"Do you remember the name of the person?" Evie asked.

"George Stevens. That set off a murmured discussion which I strained to hear because the conversation took place before I decided to wake up." Lotte smiled and gave a knowing shake of her head. "Someone called him Gory George Stevens."

"You know him," Evie exclaimed.

"Yes, indeed, I do. Or rather, I know of him. According to rumors, you do not cross Gory George because if you do, you risk turning up in the Thames. He has the reputation for being short tempered, quite nasty and quick to act against anyone he thinks has wronged him. Despite the crimes he's supposedly committed, he's never been charged."

"And this man will be attending the ball?" Henrietta asked, her eyes slightly widened with surprise and shock that she would soon be rubbing shoulders with a member of the criminal world.

"Wait a minute, I know the name." Evie swung away and began pacing. "Sterling Wright mentioned George Stevens either last night at dinner or when we arrived for the foxhunt."

"Oh, dear. Evangeline is pacing again. Share your thoughts with us and spare the carpet, please."

Evie stopped pacing. "I'm just thinking... What if Lotte is right and there is something to the way Marjorie Devon reacted when she heard his name mentioned?"

Toodles brightened. "We'll be right there to witness... Something. That will be marvelous."

"Do you know when exactly he'll be arriving?" Evie asked.

Lotte shook her head.

Evie thought about the telephone call she had made a couple of days before. She hadn't told anyone about it and no one had bothered to ask. Now she wondered if she should make another telephone call...

Tom sidled up to her. Lowering his voice, he said, "You're nibbling the edge of your lip. Is there something we should know?"

"I'll tell you later," Evie whispered.

Henrietta drew their attention back to the group. "I wish someone had mentioned *rosebud green*. It is irritating me to the point of distraction. Did anything happen after you retired for the evening?"

"I waited for everyone else to come up." Looking at Henrietta, Lotte smiled. "Yes, I had my ear pressed to the door. Twiggy Lloyd and his wife, Helena, were in the room next to mine. They argued in harsh whispers."

"What about?"

"I could only make out the insults. She called him an imbecile and said he would ruin them both."

"Sounds as if there is something happening," Toodles mused.

Evie agreed. Could those remarks be tied in with the threatening letters?

Lotte continued, "Anyhow, after an hour or so, I took a chance and stepped out."

Alarmed, Sara asked, "Oh, heavens. What were you going to say if someone saw you?"

"I had a glass with me," Lotte explained. "If I encountered anyone, I had planned on saying I'd been trying to find something to drink. And, of course, I used the glass to amplify the sounds through the doors."

Sara and Henrietta exclaimed, "You eavesdropped on the other guests? What did you hear?"

Lotte lowered her voice and whispered, "We must do something."

"Who said that?" Sara asked.

"Someone two doors down from my room. At first, I didn't know who it was because I had no idea who had been allotted to which room. So I had to wait until morning and, of course, I slept in. That forced me to sneak into the room. There are only two couples staying at Hillsboro Lodge. I already knew the Lloyd couple were next to me. Then there's Mr. and Mrs. Prentiss. But, for all I knew, it might have been Sterling Wright and Marjorie Devon. Anyhow, it finally occurred to sneak in and rummage through their clothes and, remembering what Pamela Prentiss had worn the previous evening, I found the dress and confirmed it had been them. So, why would Pamela Prentiss say they needed to do something?"

They all fell silent as they tossed around the information Lotte had shared with them.

In the midst of that silence, the main door to the house opened and Caro rushed in out of the cold.

She hurried to the fireplace and pulled her gloves off.

Everyone looked both relieved and surprised to see her.

"Thank goodness you've returned. Evangeline was about to send a posse after you."

"Heavens, I thought I'd never get away. Marjorie Devon loved the dress Mrs. Green made for her but she insisted on some alterations right there and then and, of course, I had to do them. Then she just had to try the other dress she had brought along with her and compare the two. All the while, she wouldn't stop eating and I swear she gained several pounds right before my eyes because when she tried the dress on again, it wouldn't fit so I had to do more alterations." Caro scooped in a big breath and then sighed with relief. "I'm ever so glad to be back. That woman makes me nervous. Every time she heard a motor car approaching, she would rush to the window."

Evie looked at Lotte. "Could she be nervous about George Stevens' arrival?"

Lotte gave a pensive shake of her head. "I'll need to make a telephone call to see if my contacts can tell me anything."

Evie gasped and, thinking out loud, said, "George Stevens sold Sterling Wright a horse. He thinks George wants to buy it back."

Sara looked confused. "Why would that make Marjorie Devon nervous?"

Evie tried to stitch together every other little incident they had witnessed or heard about. Were they all connected to George Stevens? "That's what we'll have to find out."

CHAPTER 11

Calm is restored

The library

om peered inside the library and found Evie sitting by the fireplace studying the road maps. "Here you are."

Evie looked up. "Heavens, I've lost track of time." After the excitement of Lotte and Caro's return, they had all sat down to lunch, agreeing to talk about anything but the last couple of days. After lunch, they had all dispersed. Henrietta and Sara had returned to the dower house, Toodles had claimed she needed to write some letters while Caro and Lotte had turned their focus to sorting out their dresses for the evening ahead.

Tom walked in, his hands in his pockets. "Where is everyone?"

"I think they're all trying to calm down. I heard Henrietta say the day is not even half over and we've had too much excitement so she needed to recoup her energy in readiness for more excitement. And I'm picking up where we left off earlier." Selecting one of the road maps, she held it out. "Here, you can make yourself useful and look through this one."

Tom chortled. "I thought I was already useful as a prop."

"I love that you can make fun of yourself," Evie mused as she followed her finger along a road on the map.

Tom settled down opposite her. After a moment of silence, he looked up. "Earlier, you were going to tell me something."

It took a moment for Evie to sift through her thoughts. Setting the map down, she drummed her fingers on it. "A couple of days ago I made a telephone call. I haven't mentioned it because at the time I felt silly. I should be able to make up my own mind but I needed some advice."

Tom gave a knowing nod. "You telephoned Detective O'Neill."

"Yes, how did you know?"

"You were grappling with the idea of becoming a lady detective."

"You don't mind?"

"You already know what I think. It makes sense to seek someone else's opinion. What did he say?"

"He encouraged me."

"You sound surprised."

"That's because I am. Part of me wanted him to say I

should stick to being a lady of leisure. However, he seems to think I have some talent and could be quite successful. Actually, he might have said useful." She drummed her fingers on the map again. "I'm still trying to decide if he put on a show of diplomacy. He buttered me up by saying I knew when to step back and contact the police."

"Have you told him about Lotte's case?"

"No, that's not something I can decide on my own. I'll have to talk it over with Lotte." She sighed. "I wonder if we should speak with him? He could tap into his contacts. Remember, there's a member of the crime world involved."

"Yes, that's been worrying me. His presence can't be a coincidence. Then again, Sterling Wright is involved in the racing world."

"Do you think it's full of bribery and corruption?"

"I think it's an easy assumption to make. There's a lot of gambling money involved so there must be an element of criminality lurking in the shadows."

"I hope the threatening letters didn't come from George Stevens."

"And if they did? How do you think he fits into the picture?" Tom asked.

"Sterling said he wanted to buy the horse back. I keep coming back to that."

"And he's not willing to sell?"

"No, he's not. And I'm going to assume George Stevens is not the type to take no for an answer."

"So the question is, what is he capable of doing to get his own way?" Tom asked.

"George Stevens might try to coerce him by force."

Tom prompted her, "And if that fails?"

Evie gave it some thought. "If I let my imagination run wild, I think I could picture George Stevens trying to enlist Marjorie Devon's help in convincing her fiancé to sell the horse."

Tom thought about it for a moment. "You wouldn't have to try hard to convince me of your theory. Do the threatening letters fit into your scenario? When Marjorie burst in with Lotte, she accused Lotte of sending the letters. That suggests she doesn't know where they originated from."

"You're right. That does rather put a dampener on my theory." In the next breath, Evie laughed. "Imagine if George Stevens proposed the idea of talking Sterling Wright into selling the horse but he avoided stating it all clearly."

"You mean, he talked in euphemisms?"

"I imagine that's what criminals do to avoid being incriminated. Anyway, he assumes his message got through to her but it didn't and Marjorie goes about her business. When it looks as if she's done nothing about his proposal, he starts sending her threatening letters as a reminder of what he is capable of."

Tom smiled. "I like it."

"Yes, but do you think it's possible?"

"Absolutely."

Evie studied him for a moment. "So it's actually possible to speak to someone and think they understand what you're saying when, in reality, they don't?"

Tom shrugged.

"Even if they give some indication they are listening?"

His eyes brimmed with amusement. A moment later, he grinned.

"Wait a minute… Have you ever listened to me talking, agreed with whatever I was saying but didn't actually understand a word I'd said?"

"Pardon?"

"You're pulling my leg." She turned her attention back to the road map. "I'm afraid we won't discover the significance of *rosebud green* until it is too late."

"Agreed."

Glancing at Tom, Evie murmured, "I'm almost tempted to ask what you just agreed to."

Smiling, he lifted the road map for a closer look. "I think I found it."

"Really?" Evie jumped out of her chair and went to stand next to Tom. "Where?"

He circled the area with his finger. "It's a small village."

"But it's nowhere near a train station." Caro had been the one to suggest rosebud green might be a place and Sara had come up with the idea it might be a place Marjorie had seen from the train during her journey from London to Hillsboro Lodge. What if she had driven from town? "How far is it from here?"

"About half an hour's drive, or thereabouts." He looked up. "Are you going to suggest we drive out there?"

Evie stared at the road map. It would be an easy drive there and back. But what did she hope to achieve? Yes, they could walk around and ask a few questions but, with no crime committed, she suspected they'd walk away empty-handed.

"We'll be getting ready to go to the Hunt Ball soon. I think that's really where we should be."

"Because you expect something will happen?"

Shrugging, Evie walked back to her chair and sat down to stare at the fireplace.

"You're fixating about something," Tom observed.

"Yes, I am. When I fret, I pace around. I'm thinking about the way Marjorie acted when Caro was there for the dress fitting."

"And you think Marjorie Devon is fretting about something and using food to calm herself down?"

Giving a small nod, she fell silent and watched the fire. She tried to clear her mind, but her thoughts kept tossing around everything, or rather, the little they knew. Despite her efforts, she couldn't shake off the feeling something was about to happen.

"This feels like the calm before the storm," Tom said.

"That's just what I was thinking. Then again, we might be getting carried away and making connections where there are none and letting our imagination lead us astray…"

"But what if?" Tom asked.

"Precisely. I keep going back to Marjorie Devon's reaction when Lotte chased her here. She accused Lotte of writing those threatening letters. It seems so outrageous. Marjorie only recently arrived in the area. Why would she think a local targeted her?"

"I want to know why her fiancé hired Lotte to follow her. Did we miss something obvious?"

Evie glanced at Tom. "He doesn't trust her?" Remembering Caro's observation, she shook her head. "Or, what if he took enough action to appease his conscience when, in fact, he'd rather shrug off the threats? As you know, I have an uncle in the newspaper business and I've heard him speak about receiving threatening mail which he never takes seriously."

"People react differently to threats."

"Indeed. And then there are people who take pre-emptive action. As far as I know, Toodles never received a threat and yet she hired you."

"True. I heard say Senator William A. Clark has a panic room built in his Fifth Avenue mansion because of the threats he receives and he never goes anywhere without a bodyguard." Tom shifted and, resting his elbow on the armrest, he cupped his chin in his hand. "Let's say something happens to Marjorie Devon. What's the first thing you'd do? Suspect someone at the house party? Would the perpetrator be so bold?"

"Are you testing me or just killing time?" she asked.

"I'd like to think I'm encouraging you."

She gave a small nod. "If you're going to create a scenario, you'll have to provide more information. How does Marjorie meet her end?"

Tom gave it some thought and then said, "In the stables. She's found with a note in her hand demanding her presence there at a certain time."

"Handwriting," Evie mused. "We'd have to look at that."

"What if the perpetrator is really smart and has thought to disguise his handwriting?" he asked.

Evie tried to remember something Detective O'Neill had said about criminals always leaving some sort of clue. "There's bound to be a way to make an identification. The pen used. The thickness of the nib. The color of the ink. The quality of the paper. The stables would provide clues too. The killer is bound to leave a footprint. Hillsboro

Lodge is a large estate. There are many workers around. I'm sure we'd be able to find a witness who saw or heard something unusual. Then, there are the guests. Someone would have noticed someone missing. I'd try to establish everyone's whereabouts." Evie smiled. "The rest would be up to the police."

Tom stretched his legs out and crossed them at the ankles. "And out of the guests we met, which one would you say is the one most likely to try to kill Marjorie?"

She said the first name that came to mind. "Twiggy Lloyd appears to have a quick temper."

"And what would be his motive?"

Evie shrugged. "Someone with a bad temper doesn't need one. Or... maybe Marjorie could say something to trigger his temper. Something about horses. Sterling Wright said Twiggy wants to partner up with him. Marjorie could make a blithe remark about him having no hope of getting what he wanted." Evie sat up. "We might need to look at this from another angle. Maybe Marjorie tried to blackmail someone."

Tom frowned. "Why would she do that? She's about to marry a wealthy man."

"For some people, too much money is not enough. Here's another theory. She has a perverse sense of right-eousness. For instance, she knows Helena Lloyd is having clandestine meetings with her lover and Marjorie disap-proves so she threatens to tell Twiggy Lloyd and provide proof of his wife's infidelity. Twiggy Lloyd knows about his wife's affairs but doesn't want anyone else to know so he kills Marjorie to shut her up. And now the more I think about it, the more I believe the police should be alerted."

"I agree. We have been made aware of a possible crime in the making and, here we are, sitting back and waiting for something to happen."

"Are you about to suggest we should try to prevent it?" Evie chortled. "There are certainly enough of us to keep an eye on everyone." She held up a finger. "The ball is tonight and George Stevens will be attending. His presence might be the element that triggers… something."

CHAPTER 12

Starry night

Hillsboro Lodge

"Did you call the detective?" Tom asked.

Evie pretended she hadn't heard. Then, she thought better of not sharing the information. "Lotte reminded me we are private lady detectives." Her instinct had been to inform the Scotland Yard detective without delay. However, without proof of a crime being committed she risked being accused of wasting his time. Not that he would ever come straight out and say that…

"How do you feel about that?"

"I doubt the detective would rush down here just

because we think something *might* happen." Sighing, Evie changed the subject. "It's a beautiful night for it."

"For the ball or for murder?" Tom asked.

She managed a chuckle. "At least, we have been kept entertained. I imagine this is how most cases will develop." She'd actually enjoyed tossing ideas around with Tom—something she looked forward to doing in the future.

Of course, she had to admit, some of the ideas had been rather convoluted. But they had helped by providing them with more possibilities.

Pointing ahead, she said, "The ball is well under way." With all the lights on, the house could be seen from a distance. Two other motor cars drove ahead of them. "It's strange, I only just realized there will be other guests besides the ones we met."

"More people to suspect."

"Yes, indeed."

Earlier, Henrietta and Sara had driven up to Halton House for an early supper, something they had suggested doing saying once they arrived at the ball they might not have the opportunity to sit down to a meal.

"Are we all expecting something dreadful to happen? Heavens, it feels as if we're trying to rack up business."

Tom grinned. "Yes, it does. What do you have to say for yourself, Countess? Do you think your credibility will suffer if nothing happens?"

"I'm quite happy to be proven wrong."

Tom slowed down and waited for the motor car ahead of them to clear the way. Tapping his fingers on the steering wheel, he said, "We don't have a description of George Stevens."

"Identifying him will be our first priority. I'm sure someone will be only too happy to point him out to us."

"You're convinced he's here to make trouble."

"According to Lotte, he is a slippery fellow and doesn't like being out in public. Yet here he is."

"This is not exactly a public arena."

"Granted, this is a private event but I doubt he knows every guest attending and vice versa. I suppose he might think he can enjoy the night without being recognized."

Evie adjusted her coat and smiled at the fact they had all chosen to wear black or gray. Congregating in the hall at Halton House, there had been a moment of silence as they'd each scrutinized everyone's gown.

Explaining her choice, Henrietta had said, "We'll want to blend in."

"Yes, we can't afford to draw attention to ourselves," Sara had agreed.

Evie studied the motor car ahead of them. "Is that a Rolls Royce?"

"Yes."

She couldn't remember any of the local gentry owning such an extravagant motor car. The chauffeur jumped out and opened the door to a stocky looking man dressed in tails. He, in turn, held his hand out to his companion. The woman who stepped out of the motor car had platinum blonde hair and a silver coat. Evie thought she caught a glimpse of something quite glittery.

"Does that man look like a criminal?" she asked.

"Now, now, Countess. We mustn't jump to conclusions and judge by appearances."

"No, indeed, we mustn't. However, I can't help it. He looks suspicious. Henrietta's eyes must be bulging out."

The Rolls Royce moved on, making way for Evie and Tom.

He jumped out of the roadster, rounding it to open the door for her.

Sterling Wright had a full complement of staff, including footmen dressed in blue and gold livery. While it definitely confirmed his wealth, in Evie's opinion, it also showed a degree of ostentation since, in her experience, only members of the highest ranks of nobility went to such lengths. Although, back home, Mrs. Astor had been in the habit of having her servants dressed in livery and she hadn't been in possession of a title.

Evie hoped Sterling Wright didn't feel he needed to impress people. She knew for a fact most locals would just be glad someone had taken up residence since an empty manor house equaled people out of work.

"I never actually asked," Tom said. "What happens at a hunt ball? I'm getting images of men sporting stag heads or fox tails."

"I think that's called a masquerade ball and, in answer to your question, it's just a ball to celebrate the end of the foxhunting season."

"So it's an annual event."

As they walked toward the entrance, she glanced at him. "Are you trying to picture the future to come?"

"I might have to. Otherwise, it'll just keep catching me by surprise."

Walking in, they saw guests milling about the great hall with its massive stone fireplace, paneled walls, an impressive chandelier, dozens of candles, as well as massive paintings of horses and hunting scenes. A lively jazz tune wafted from the adjoining ballroom. Despite the formal setting, the mood for the evening appeared to be relaxed.

Glancing over her shoulder, Evie wondered what Sara and Henrietta would make of it all. She saw them walk across the graveled entrance and step inside, their eyes bright with excitement.

Greeting them, the butler helped Evie out of her coat. As she thanked him, Sterling Wright approached them and welcomed them.

"Lady Woodridge, I'm sure you're accustomed to a receiving line. I'm afraid I've broken with protocol and adopted a more relaxed approach."

Evie noticed the butler lifting his imperious nose. No doubt there would be some talk of it downstairs.

Smiling, Evie looked for Marjorie Devon but did not see her.

"She's around somewhere," Sterling explained. "Most likely dancing. She organized the band to start playing even before the first guest arrived."

While Sterling Wright moved on to greet more guests, Henrietta and the others joined them.

"Mingle and observe," Evie whispered.

Henrietta and Sara passed on the message to Caro, Toodles and Lotte who were already busy looking around.

They had a simple strategy. They would move around and watch how Marjorie Devon interacted with everyone. Lotte had said they needed to pay particular attention to anyone she might appear to be avoiding.

Moving along the great hall, Evie and Tom smiled and nodded, greeting everyone as they continued walking until they reached the end of the hall. They stood there watching the others spreading out and doing just as they had planned.

Caro looked elegant in a smoky gray ensemble with matching headband. She accepted a drink and proceeded to work her way from one group to the other.

"Furtive glances," Caro had suggested earlier, "We must be on the lookout for those and spare no one."

Hearing her, Tom had laughed. "The net widens. Let's hope there isn't a crime committed. Can you imagine what it would take to round up all these suspects?"

At first, Henrietta and Sara worked together talking with one person and then another while Toodles went her own way.

Evie watched her granny put her strategy into place by positioning herself so she could eavesdrop on people's conversations.

Meanwhile, Lotte had headed straight for the ballroom.

"Ready?" Tom asked.

"Instead of working our way around, I think we should start with letting people come to us," Evie suggested. "And use this vantage point to keep an eye on everyone here. There's no hurry. Lotte is taking care of the ballroom."

Tom looked around the great hall. "The entrance halls in these large houses still mystify me. I fail to see why they are so large when the owners seem to spend so little time in them."

Evie followed his gaze. "I know what you mean. The great hall at Halton House only comes alive during cele-brations. Mostly, during Christmas when we put the tree and decorations up." She saw Twiggy Lloyd and his wife heading toward the ballroom. Looking around the hall again, she added, "When the houses were first erected, the halls were used by the entire household. Both the owners and servants used to eat there. Then, a couple of hundred years ago, the eating arrangements changed and now we all eat in separate spaces."

"Well, that answers that."

When a footman approached with a tray of drinks, Evie scooped in a breath.

"We should abstain but it would look too obvious. If you hear me slur my words, please take the glass away from me."

"Ditto."

They were approached by a couple who recognized them from the foxhunt. Evie repeated their names three times and, a moment later, found she couldn't remember them so she mentally thought of them as Mrs. Red for her gown, and Mr. Pearl Tie Pin.

Smiling at something Mrs. Red Dress said, Evie took the opportunity to let her gaze wander across the hall. The couple had only recently been introduced to Sterling Wright, so Evie assumed they would have nothing whatsoever to do with sending threatening letters to his fiancée.

Joined by another couple, Evie named the woman Mauve, for her dress, and her husband, Crooked Tie. Halfway through the conversation, which focused on an approaching storm, Mrs. Red Dress and her husband, Mr. Pearl Tie Pin, responded to the tune of their favorite dance music and excused themselves.

All the while, Evie's gaze bounced around from side to side, group to group and then back to Sterling Wright. He hovered near the entrance greeting his guests. Despite the ball being in full swing, there continued to be an endless stream of people arriving. Evie recognized some but not all the guests.

Subjecting everyone to a skating scrutiny, Evie didn't sense any suspicious behavior. Smiling to herself, she wondered when she had begun thinking of herself as an expert in defining behavior.

People's gazes wavered, drifted, focused, and then continued on around the hall and, Evie noticed, always returned to Sterling Wright.

Did she find that unusual? No because she had been doing precisely that. As the host, it made sense for him to be the point of everyone's attention.

The next couple who approached them were also concerned about the approaching storm, expected to reach the area the next day. When another couple expressed the same concerns, Evie decided the weather had become a safe talking point for anyone who'd otherwise have nothing else to say because they feared saying something that might offend.

Tom leaned in and whispered, "Do you see anything interesting?"

"Not really but I'm learning a great deal about observing. It's rather difficult. All I have to do is look. But my mind keeps interfering with ridiculous thoughts."

Tom sighed. "Your library contains some books on Eastern philosophy and something called meditation. You might need to practice quietening your mind."

Evie gave him a worried look.

"What? Did I say something strange?"

"Not strange. Merely unexpected. This is where I say there is much to learn about you, Mr. Winchester."

Caro emerged from the ballroom and sought them out. However, instead of heading straight for them, she wove her way around, smiling and chatting briefly with the guests she encountered along the way.

"You do that extremely well, Cousin Carolina," Evie said when Caro finally reached them. "You're like a butterfly in a flower garden, fleeting about. I hadn't even realized you'd stepped inside the ballroom."

"This is hard work. I have been keeping the conversations brief, especially after encountering a couple of people who recognized me but couldn't quite place me." Accepting a glass of champagne, Caro lifted the glass to her lips but did not drink. "I thought you might want to know Mr. George Stevens arrived an hour ago and has spent all this time dancing with his wife."

So, the couple who had arrived just before them had not been George Stevens and his companion. "What does he look like?" Evie asked.

Caro tilted her head in thought. "He's not what we expected. He's clean-shaven with light brown thinning hair, spectacles and delicate features."

"What about his wife? What color dress is she wearing?"

"Purple with light blue trim." Caro took a small sip of her champagne. "Marjorie Devon is wearing Mrs. Green's pink creation. She hasn't stopped dancing either."

"Who is she dancing with?"

"Every man she can get to dance with her. She's already worn out a couple of them. And, no, she hasn't danced with George Stevens. In fact, I couldn't help noticing she has kept her distance. It's too obvious for it to be a coincidence. I might even go so far as to say they are playing a cat and mouse game. Whenever George Stevens comes close to her, she performs a quick step away from him, even if it isn't part of the dance routine."

Tom took Evie's champagne glass and, catching the attention of a footman, he set their glasses on a tray. "Shall we move to the dance floor?"

Hesitating, Evie took a deep swallow. "The ballroom?"

"That's where all the action seems to be."

Evie glanced around the hall. Henrietta and Sara were nowhere to be seen so she assumed they were in the ballroom. "But the others are already there. Wouldn't it be better if we stay here and keep an eye on..." She floundered.

Taking her hand, Tom led her into the ballroom. "A spin around for credibility," he suggested.

Evie looked over her shoulder and took mental images of everyone standing in the hall. "I... I don't spin very well." She loved music and she enjoyed watching people dancing but, right now, her mind was filled with other thoughts. "It's a foxtrot. Maybe we should sit this one out." Too many steps mingling with too many thoughts were bound to end in embarrassment.

"Nonsense. This is just the type of dance that can get us to our target quickly." He frowned. "What's wrong? Am I about to learn something about you that I didn't know before?" Slipping his hand along the small of her back, Tom swept her onto the dance floor. "Follow the rhythm of the music."

Evie looked one way and the other trying to place everyone. "I'll try." She kept up with Tom, while at the same time trying to keep Marjorie in sight. In the process, she missed several steps. If Tom noticed, he didn't say anything.

"Where did she go?"

Tom swung her around. "Over my left shoulder now."

Evie searched the couples dancing until she found Marjorie Devon. She also spotted a few familiar faces including Matthew and Pamela Prentiss and Twiggy Lloyd and his wife. She identified George Stevens—the only man she could see wearing glasses. Keeping track of him, she noticed him guiding his wife toward Marjorie. Caro had been right. He certainly didn't look like a criminal. In fact, he reminded her of a clerk working in an office, albeit one dressed in formal clothes.

The music ended and before Tom could drag her into the next dance, she pulled him away from the dance floor.

"Let's sit this one out. There are many things I can juggle but not dancing and thinking."

"Can you imagine what Lotte will do if she hears about that?"

"She'll probably make me practice for hours on end. Let's keep it to ourselves, shall we?" Turning, she looked for Marjorie. "Oh, where is she?"

"Actually, where's George Stevens?"

CHAPTER 13

Missing in action

"*W*here's Lotte?"

The band started playing another piece and everyone converged on the dance floor. Everyone except Marjorie Devon and George Stevens. They still hadn't returned.

Evie swung around trying to place the other couples she'd seen. "Where is Matthew Prentiss?" She'd seen Matthew Prentiss and his wife, Pamela, among the throng of people swirling around the dance floor. Had they taken a break?

"I don't know, I'm searching for Twiggy and Helena Lloyd." Taking her hand, Tom led the way around the ballroom. "They were all here a moment ago."

They wove their way back to where they had started.

"Perhaps they went out to the hall," Tom suggested.

Declining an offer of more champagne, they left the ballroom and headed back to the great hall. The same people who had been there before were still there, clearly intent on conversing rather than dancing. However, the people they had noticed missing were still missing.

Seeing Caro, Evie headed straight for her. Lowering her voice to a whisper, she asked, "Have you seen Marjorie?"

"Yes, she came through a moment ago."

Relief swept through Evie. "Where did she go?"

"Upstairs. Lotte followed at a discreet distance."

Evie asked about the others but Caro hadn't seen them.

Nodding, Caro said, "I've been doing my best to keep track of people."

"You're definitely doing a better job of it. We've lost everyone." Turning, Evie searched for Sterling and found him chatting with a group of guests. "That's one less person to worry about," she murmured.

Tom nudged her. "I think Henrietta and Sara are still in the ballroom but I don't see Toodles."

"Let's hope she followed someone." Belatedly, she wished they had set some firm rules about taking precautions.

Asking Caro to remain in the hall, Evie led the way toward the dining room. They found a few guests milling about the table which had been set up with large platters of food.

"No sign of Toodles and still no sign of the others."

"Outside?" Tom asked.

"Why would anyone go outside? It's too cold."

"One of the drawing rooms?"

They moved from room to room and ended up in the library. Walking straight toward the welcoming fire, Evie tried to clear her head.

"Is it time to worry?" Evie stared at the empty room. Where had they all disappeared to?

"I'm sure there's a simple explanation. This is a party and... unusual things happen."

Finding no comfort in the explanation, Evie asked, "Such as?"

Tom looked around the library. "It's a large house. With so many guests, some of them might have decided to go exploring."

"Some of them? You mean, the ones we'd been keeping an eye on."

"Yes, that is strange."

"And why now? What did we miss? Who made the first move? Did someone leave the ballroom first and did the others follow?"

Tom walked up to a window. Shifting the curtain aside, he looked outside. "Are you thinking out loud? I hope you are because I don't have any answers for you."

"They're not going to miraculously appear so I guess we should continue searching for them."

Heading back to the hall, she breathed a sigh of relief. When she spoke, the words nearly caught in her throat. "I see Henrietta and Sara. I know they remained in the ballroom. It's just a relief to see them safe and sound."

Tom pointed to the far end. "And there's Toodles."

As if by silent consensus, they all turned to look at Evie and Tom.

"They're just as surprised to see us." Evie turned and looked toward the stairs. "Lotte is still missing."

"No." Tom nudged his head toward the ballroom.

Lotte stood at the doorway looking around. Seeing Tom and Evie, she walked toward them, along the way accepting a glass of champagne.

Sounding slightly out of breath, she said, "I lost Marjorie Devon."

"But you followed her upstairs." How could everyone disappear so suddenly?

"Yes, I did follow her, and I saw her go inside her room." Lotte adjusted her monocle. "I lingered out of sight. She finally came out and headed down the servants' staircase. That's when I lost her."

Henrietta, Sara and Toodles joined them in time to hear Lotte's account.

Before Evie could ask where they had disappeared to, Henrietta said, "When the music finished, we noticed the Prentiss couple making their way out of the ballroom so we followed at a discreet distance. When I saw Matthew Prentiss looking over his shoulder, we stopped to admire some paintings. That happened a couple of times and finally we lost sight of them. We thought they went inside one of the drawing rooms. But when we stepped inside, they were gone. Sara rushed to the window but she didn't see anyone."

"Good heavens," Evie exclaimed. "Tom and I thought you were both in the ballroom. You mean to say you were missing too?"

Henrietta looked puzzled. "No, we knew where we were all along."

Glancing over Sara's shoulder, Evie saw Matthew Prentiss and his wife, Pamela, emerging from the ball-room. They stopped to take drinks from a footman and then joined a group of people. Evie breathed a sigh of relief. "I see two of them."

The others followed her gaze.

"This is interesting," Tom murmured. "There's Twiggy Lloyd and his wife."

"Yes, and his cheeks are red." Sending her gaze skating around the hall, she saw Sterling Wright emerging through a side door and looking quite stern. "And there's someone I hadn't noticed missing. He must have slipped out when we weren't looking." She followed the direction of Sterling's gaze. It led her straight to Twiggy Lloyd.

Had they been arguing again?

Evie searched for the others. "Who else did we notice missing?"

"George Stevens." Tom checked his watch. "How much time do you think we spent searching for them?"

Evie couldn't really say.

"Half an hour?" Tom suggested. "Did anyone notice the time?"

No one had.

"What now?" Toodles asked. "Do we try to find out where they went?"

"Even if they're willing to tell you, there's no way to confirm what they say," Lotte mused. "There are still some other people missing. Marjorie and George Stevens." She turned to leave only to stop when she saw Marjorie Devon standing with her husband.

"Is she wearing a different dress?" Evie asked. "I'm sure I saw her wearing a pink dress."

"That's the blue dress she brought with her," Caro said.

Evie turned and gasped. She had actually lost sight of Caro but she'd been standing next to her all along.

Caro continued, "I remember she tried it on and wanted some adjustments made to it."

Why had she changed her gown? Had she spilled something on her pink dress?

"It explains why she went upstairs," Tom offered.

Evie turned to Lotte. "Did you notice her wearing a different dress?"

"No, in fact, when she came out of her room, she was wearing the pink dress. I remember thinking the color didn't really suit her."

"Are you sure?"

"I'm not the best judge, but not everyone can carry that pale shade of pink."

Evie puzzled over Lotte's response. "I meant, are you sure she was wearing pink. Never mind, you already answered the question. Albeit in a roundabout way."

So, Evie thought, at some point, after Lotte had lost her, Marjorie Devon had returned to her room and changed into the blue dress.

What had happened to make her do that?

"Maybe she just decided she wanted to change," Caro suggested. "When Mrs. Green and I brought the pink dress for her to try on, Marjorie hadn't been able to decide which one she would wear to the ball. Perhaps she realized she could actually wear both."

That sounded like a reasonable explanation. Evie watched Lotte weave her way back to the ballroom. A moment later, she returned, her expression blank.

"George Stevens isn't back yet."

"What about his wife?"

Lotte shook her head.

"Perhaps they left." Evie turned to Tom.

"I'll go out and have a chat with the chauffeurs."

Evie tried to remember who else was staying at the house. "Oh, what about Archie Arthurs? Has anyone seen him?"

"Who?" Toodles asked.

Evie described him. "Stocky with stooped shoulders. No experience on horses."

"Stocky like Twiggy Lloyd?"

"Yes, I suppose so. Anyhow, he's one of the other guests staying here."

No one remembered seeing a man fitting that description. It seemed odd to attend the foxhunt and then forego the final event.

"We appear to be the only ones in a state of panic," Henrietta observed.

"I wouldn't necessarily say we have panicked," Sara argued even as she pressed her hand to her chest. "Although, I must admit, my imagination is running wild."

"What with?" Henrietta asked.

"With images of what might have happened. Think about it. One moment, everyone was in the ballroom dancing and, the next moment, they all disappeared. Did you notice anyone else leaving? No. Only those staying at the house."

Evie wished they had some way of finding out who'd left first and…

If the others had followed.

Caro gave her sleeve a tug. "I've lost sight of Matthew Prentiss and his wife. I'm going to the ballroom."

A glance around the hall almost made Evie dizzy. "Where's Marjorie Devon?"

Henrietta and Sara piped in, "We've lost Twiggy Lloyd again."

Before she could stop them, the dowagers went in search of Twiggy Lloyd with Toodles trailing after them.

Evie groaned under her breath. "I suppose I should stay here." Catching the attention of a footman, she helped herself to a glass of champagne. Taking a sip, she changed her mind. "The night is not over yet," she murmured.

CHAPTER 14

Lost and found and lost again

The great hall
Hillsboro Lodge

*R*elief swept through Evie when she saw Tom returning from talking with the chauffeurs. Evie tried to read his expression but he did a splendid job of hiding his thoughts as he wove his way toward her smiling and greeting people so she had no way of telling if he brought good news or bad news.

Along the way, he picked up a couple of champagne glasses. He handed Evie a glass and stood by watching the guests as he took a sip of his drink. His tactic tested Evie's patience. Finally, he said, "All the motor cars are still here. No one's left yet."

Where could they have gone? "Everyone who'd returned has disappeared again. Do you think they're having a private meeting somewhere?" Evie looked past Tom's shoulder. Sterling Wright stood with a group of guests chatting and laughing.

Everyone continued to enjoy themselves. Lively music wafted from the ballroom. "We must be making too big a deal of it. Either that or there is something strange going on right under our noses."

Tom cast his gaze around the gathering. "There's definitely something wrong here."

"It's possible they just went wandering around the house. Whenever I'm a guest in a new house, I like to explore the picture galleries." Although, that didn't explain Marjorie Devon's absence earlier.

Tom grinned. "You mean, you like to snoop."

Putting on a haughty tone, Evie lifted her chin. "I like to admire and appreciate. That's the reason why people have so many works of art and fine furniture on display. Besides, I'm not the only one. Henrietta and Sara also enjoy wandering around."

"They did that because they were following the Prentiss couple. Actually, where are the others?"

"They went exploring. At least, that's the excuse they'll give if anyone asks."

"I suppose the dowagers and Toodles will look less suspicious." He raised his glass to his lips. "And I'm sure Caro can talk her way out of anything. If you change your mind about becoming a lady detective, you could turn your attention to becoming a society thief. You already have your band of adventure seeking would-be thieves."

"Mr. Winchester, I'm shocked that you would even propose such a venture."

"Are you?"

Evie shifted and smiled. "Actually, I'm not at all surprised by the suggestion or the fact that I spent a moment entertaining the idea. Of course, it would never work. We simply don't have it in us."

He gave a pensive nod. "Lotte didn't exactly come straight out and say it, but I believe you need a creative mind for the job at hand."

"Are you trying to distract me?"

"Yes, you're fixating. I thought you might help to think about something else."

Evie hummed under her breath. "No, I can't quite see myself walking around in disguise."

He lifted an eyebrow and teased her, "Really? I think you would have no trouble disguising yourself as an indigent, half-crazed woman."

Evie gave him a measuring look. "And I think you would do just fine playing the role of my husband."

Tom grinned.

"Or my butler." Evie shrugged. "We already know you can fool everyone as a chauffeur."

"Brace yourself," Tom murmured, "Sterling Wright is heading straight for us."

Smiling, Evie greeted him. "Your ball has been a wonderful success."

He rocked on the heels of his feet. "Ah, yes. And yet, I'm slightly disappointed because no one has danced on a table. I doubt the event will make the society pages."

"Few country events do." Unless something happened, Evie thought. "Also, these days, we're competing with the bright young things."

"At least it was well attended."

"I think you'll find us country folk all quite enthusiastic. You might want to see about holding a garden party or a fête for the local village. They'll really appreciate that."

He raised a glass to the idea.

Evie took the opportunity to ask, "Did George Stevens approach you about buying back the horse?"

Sterling gave her a brisk smile. "Not yet. I'm sure he's biding his time and he'll have plenty of it since he's spending a couple of days here." Suddenly, his attention drifted away.

Evie saw the butler standing nearby.

Giving a nod, Sterling said, "You must excuse me. It appears I am needed elsewhere."

Once he was out of hearing, Tom asked, "Is Sterling Wright looking to make a name for himself as the host of the season?"

Evie watched Sterling Wright's progress across the crowded hall. His butler spoke briefly and then led the way out through a side door. "I think he might want to impress the folks back home. Unfortunately for him, he's unlikely to succeed since the only news reports that make it across are all about the success of debutantes landing a titled gentleman."

"Did you make headlines when you married the Earl of Woodridge?" Tom asked.

"Yes, of course. Although, by then, the novelty had worn off. Others before me had made bigger splashes." However, Evie thought, only a few of them had married for love. "Oh, thank goodness. I see the dowagers and Toodles. I wonder if they discovered anything of interest?"

Doing their best to remain inconspicuous, they took their time reaching them so Evie assumed their search had yielded nothing of real interest.

Henrietta's eyes twinkled with mischief. "We have been poking around the place. Sterling Wright has a descent art collection and some beautifully furnished rooms. He must have acquired some pieces at auction as I recognize some of the furniture from nearby Hertfords-by-the-field House." Lowering her voice, she murmured, "The owners lost their only son and heir. Poor souls, they put on a brave front but apparently could no longer bear living in the house without him. Then, there was only so much furniture they could fit into their London house. With no heir, their future looks dim. It's comforting to know Halton House has been spared such a fate."

"I think Evie wants to know if we found anything of interest." Sara smiled. "We encountered a maid and I asked if George Stevens' wife had retired for the night. She confirmed it. So that's one person accounted for."

"You left out the most important part," Toodles said. "The maid emerged from Marjorie Devon's room. How do we know? She was carrying her pink dress to mend."

"So that's why Marjorie changed her dress." Evie glanced at Marjorie who, surprisingly, had remained in the hall. So much for her keen desire to dance the night away. "Did Caro go with you?"

Looking worried, Henrietta adjusted her necklace. "No, she didn't. I thought she remained here with you."

"I don't like the look of this," Tom said.

"What?"

He signaled toward a side entrance.

Sterling Wright walked toward them, his face devoid of any expression, his movements steady and determined.

"Oh, heavens," Henrietta exclaimed. "I hope we're not in trouble for wandering around the house unescorted."

Avoiding eye contact with Evie and the others, Sterling Wright looked straight at Tom. Drawing him aside, he murmured something.

Tom turned to Evie. His face had drained of color. Leaning in, he whispered. "It's… Caro."

Evie's heart gave an alarming thump against her chest. Somehow, she managed to keep her voice steady. "What's happened?"

Instead of answering, he turned to the others. "We'll be back shortly." He took Evie's hand and led the way.

"What is happening?" Henrietta demanded and was echoed by the others who followed Tom and Evie.

The butler walked ahead of them. Reaching a door behind the staircase, he opened it. "We didn't think we should move her upstairs yet. The doctor has been summoned. One of the maids found her outside."

A flurry of questions swept through Evie but she couldn't find the words to express them.

They hurried down the stairs. Realizing the others had followed, Evie managed to turn and say, "Henrietta, perhaps you should all remain upstairs."

"Out of the question."

"Then please take care coming down the stairs. We don't want someone else injured."

A footman carrying a tray hurried up the stairs. When he saw them, he stood aside to let them through.

Reaching the landing, the butler signaled to a room just off the kitchen. "This is my office."

Tom and Evie rushed in and found Caro stretched out on a leather sofa.

The housekeeper stood by while a maid pressed a cloth to Caro's cheek.

Finding her voice, Evie asked, "Is she responsive?" Before anyone could answer, she kneeled down beside her and took her hand. "Caro, can you hear me?"

When the maid removed the cloth to dampen it in a bowl, Evie gasped. Caro's cheek looked red and slightly swollen. Had someone struck her? Or had Caro run into something?

Patting her hand lightly, Evie tried again. "Caro, you must say something to let us know you are fine." She had to be. Evie couldn't think of any other outcome. She didn't dare. Her thoughts had frozen in place. She couldn't even entertain the possibility of anything being other than fine.

A swirl of emotions pressed against her chest then dove all the way down to the pit of her stomach, swelling into something hard.

Tom rested his hand on Evie's shoulder and squeezed. "She will be fine. Whatever happened, I think she's just responded by going into shock."

Evie sensed movement behind her and knew the others had finally come in. Henrietta's breath whooshed out and Sara emitted a soft moan.

"Has anyone tried smelling salts?" Toodles asked.

"We didn't dare," the housekeeper said. "The doctor should be along shortly. He doesn't live very far."

"What was she doing outside?" Evie murmured and

looked up at Tom. She could feel her eyes stinging with an urgent demand for him to offer answers that made sense but he only gave a small nod before withdrawing from the room. Evie knew he had gone in search of those answers she'd demanded.

Lotte came to stand beside Evie. Leaning down, she whispered, "She will be fine."

Evie gave a stiff nod.

When Lotte moved away, Evie knew she had gone out to join Tom in his search. Between them, she hoped they would be able to find out what had happened.

Evie looked up at the housekeeper. "I'm sure Mr. Wright has already asked you. Did any of the downstairs servants see anything or hear something out of the ordinary?"

The housekeeper, dressed in severe black, stood with her hands clasped. Evie saw her press her fingers together and draw her eyebrows down as if in thought.

"We were all so very busy, my lady. It tends to become quite noisy in the kitchen." She shook her head. "One of the maids went outside and that's when she found her."

Managing to keep her voice steady, Evie asked, "Where? Right near the door?"

"No, she was near the wood-fire building. It's attached to one of the storage outhouses."

"And what else is out there?"

"There's a servant entrance and the kitchen door and…"

"I mean, are there other buildings beyond the wood-fire building?"

"The old coach house, the stables and the motor car garage are opposite. The chauffeur lives upstairs."

"Is he there now?"

"No, my lady. He's been in the kitchen all evening. Although, he stepped out a couple of times to chat with the other chauffeurs."

"And where are they?"

"They're all with their vehicles out the front."

Caro's lips parted and she moaned.

The others moved closer.

"Did she just moan?" Sara asked. "That must be a good sign, surely."

Evie had no idea how much time had passed. Someone put their hand on her shoulder and urged her to move.

"It's the doctor. He's here, Birdie."

Looking up, it took her a moment to recognize Toodles.

"Birdie. You need to give him some space."

Although reluctant, she released Caro's hand, straightened and stepped back.

The doctor set his case down and took Caro's pulse. Then, he inspected her reddened cheek. When he touched Caro's nose, she winced and moaned again. "It looks like she has been struck in the face. A blow to the nose would be enough to knock anyone out," he explained.

Someone had struck Caro? Scooping in a determined breath, Evie looked at the others. "You stay with her."

Understanding, Toodles nodded.

"Promise me you'll stay and if anything changes send someone to fetch me. I'll be outside."

Before she could change her mind, Evie swung around and found her way out. Seeing her coming, maids and footmen stepped out of the way.

"Which way to the back door?" Evie asked a maid. If

the young girl's expression was any indication, Evie had just succeeded in frightening her with her abrupt manner. Distraught and feeling utterly helpless, she apologized.

Pointing her in the right direction, the maid stepped back only to find the courage to hurry ahead and open the door for Evie.

The crisp night air engulfed Evie but it didn't deter her. She'd hoped to find Tom and Lotte out here but, at first glance, she failed to locate them.

Light from the windows spilled out lighting the immediate cobblestoned area. Stepping away from the door, she looked around and identified the outbuildings the housekeeper had mentioned.

A light moving across a window of one of the buildings caught her attention. A moment later, two figures emerged from the building carrying a lantern.

Tom and Lotte.

Seeing her, Tom asked, "How is Caro?"

"The doctor is with her." Evie wrapped her arms around her waist and shook her head. "I had to come out and… do something."

"I'm afraid we haven't found anything out here. We might have better luck in the daylight." Signaling with the lantern, Tom added, "We were just going to look around the stables and garage."

"I'll join you."

Tom handed Lotte the lantern and removed his coat. "Here, put this on."

Evie didn't bother protesting. The warmth of his coat offered her enough comfort for her to realize she had been cold.

She spoke as if in a daze. "I've been thinking… Caro

must have followed someone outside. She didn't just come out here to look around."

Both Tom and Lotte agreed.

"She must have been standing in the person's way," Lotte said. "Or, we think she might have caught someone by surprise. Someone making their way back to the house."

Evie tried to picture the scene but her mind only provided a blurred image. "From doing what?"

Lotte shrugged. "I assume there are still people missing inside. They have to be somewhere on the property."

"Maybe George Stevens and Archie Arthurs are working on a deal," Evie suggested. "Something illegal." Archie Arthurs hadn't made an appearance at the ball and George Stevens hadn't returned since the first time he'd stepped out of the ballroom.

"And you think Caro got in the way?"

Heaven help them, Evie thought. She would make sure they received the harshest penalties for their transgression.

They turned and headed toward the stables.

Evie looked down to watch where she stepped on the uneven cobblestones. "If they think Caro can identify them, then her life is in peril."

They reached the stables and peered inside. Tom walked in and lit another lantern. Instead of walking all the way in, he stopped at the entrance and held up the lantern. "I don't think we should go any further. Just in case something has happened. The flagstones are covered with straw and we might disturb it."

Had someone come out here? To do what?

Evie pointed toward the closest stall. She thought she could see a plaque. "Can you shine the lantern on the door, please?"

"Mighty Warrior," Tom read.

"That's the horse Sterling Wright just purchased. But I don't see him. Light the way for me, please." Evie walked up to the stall on tiptoes. She could just make out the shape of the horse. When it snorted, she spoke gently to it, "It's only us, Mighty Warrior. We just want to have a closer look." The horse snorted again and bobbed its head up and down. "He's in the corner. There's something odd about that. Bring the lantern closer, please."

Tom went to stand beside her. As he held the lantern up, they both leaned in.

Evie gasped. "Is… is that a man?"

CHAPTER 15

Murder and mayhem

The stables

They looked on in stunned silence for no longer than a few seconds but those seconds seemed to drag on.

Evie forced herself to move past her shock at the same time as the others and they all jumped into action.

"We must see if he's still alive."

Mighty Warrior snorted and shifted from side to side.

"One of us has to keep an eye on the horse," Lotte said.

Tom stepped forward. "That should be me."

"Heavens, my first instinct is to remove him from the stall

as quickly as possible but what if we disturb the scene?" Evie knew they needed to alert Sterling Wright and the police but their first priority had to be to get him out of the stall.

"Are you suggesting this is the scene of a crime?" Lotte asked, her tone bewildered.

With Caro injured and now a man presumably dead… Evie nodded. "We have to assume it is. I'm surprised you don't think so."

Lotte shook her head when she said, "This might come as a surprise to you but my lady detective's agency deals mostly with petty crimes."

"Evie's right." Tom agreed. "But we have to get him out of there."

Moving with care, Tom went into the stall. While he talked to the horse in a soothing tone, Lotte and Evie moved swiftly taking hold of the man's arms and dragging him out of the stall.

Neither one spoke but they both knew the identity of the man straightaway.

Backing out of the stall, Tom eased the door closed, slid the latch into place and turned it down to secure it.

"Does he have a pulse?" he asked.

Evie shook her head. "I can't feel it. One of us will have to go back inside and alert Sterling Wright. Also, the doctor should still be there." Evie only then realized she'd been in shock. "Why didn't I think of that before? We came out here looking for something… someone, we should have been prepared for the worst." Without consulting the others, she rushed out of the stables and made her way across the yard.

Bursting inside, her mere presence caught everyone's

attention. Looks were exchanged and a feeling of panic swept through the corridors.

Focused on reaching the butler's room, Evie managed to catch only glimpses of people's expressions and they all looked bewildered. Given enough time, Evie knew they would realize something had happened.

They would certainly have a lot to talk about in the morning, Evie thought.

Stumbling into the butler's room, she found Caro sitting up and sipping a cup of tea with the dowagers standing by while the doctor spoke to Toodles.

Evie pressed her hand to her chest. Her relief at seeing Caro had recovered mingled with the urgency of the moment. "Doctor."

Everyone turned to look at her.

"Good heavens. What's happened?" Henrietta demanded.

Evie gave a stiff nod. "Definitely something." She gestured to the doctor. "Please, you must hurry." Along the way, she explained, "We found a man collapsed in one of the stalls." And, she thought, someone would have the difficult task of informing the man's wife.

When they arrived at the stables, it took mere seconds for the doctor to shake his head and declare Gory George Stevens dead.

They all stepped back to take in the scene and try to make sense of it.

George Stevens had come out here and had met with death.

Had he died of natural causes?

There were no obvious injuries. With so many people

absent from the ball, Evie had no trouble imagining the worst.

She scooped in a calming breath but she still felt on edge. First, there had been Caro's attack and now this.

"Countess?" Tom murmured.

Evie recognized the prompt as Tom's way of getting her to walk him through her thought processes. He knew she was in the midst of entertaining a myriad of suspicions.

Had George Stevens come out to say hello to his horse? What could have been going through his mind? Had he planned to steal the horse?

Had someone followed him?

For what reason? To stop George Stevens? The only person who'd want to do that would be Sterling Wright and he had remained inside. Except for one brief moment, Evie thought...

Evie persevered with the idea someone had followed George Stevens out here.

The thought took hold of her and refused to let go.

She would bet anything that same person would most likely also be responsible for attacking Caro.

Detective Inspector O'Neill had once told her criminals always left something behind at the scene of a crime and, most importantly, they took something away.

An investigator needed to discover the traces left behind and make the connections. If something criminal had taken place here, the police would look for material evidence. But only if they had reason to investigate. Only if they found the death to be suspicious.

There would be a post mortem. Once they determined

the cause of death, the police would decide how to proceed. Until then...

Evidence could be lost.

Evie assured herself the police, once they arrived, would take in the scene and do a thorough search to collect evidence.

Lotte kneeled down to take a closer look at George Stevens. Evie watched her getting even closer and sniffing him.

"I would advise against touching the deceased," the doctor warned.

Although visibly reluctant, Lotte stood up and stepped back.

There had to be something here to explain what had happened. Holding on to her suspicions, Evie looked around and then fixed her attention on the stall.

Closing her eyes, she retraced their steps. Everything had happened so quickly. When they'd seen the body inside the stall, they'd known it would have to be retrieved. Tom had stepped forward to keep the horse calm but first...

He'd opened the door.

Evie looked at Tom. "The latch."

He nodded. "I had to slide it to open the stall door."

Had George Stevens slid it back into place after entering the stall and why had he gone in?

Tom brushed his hand across his chin. "It hadn't just been slid into place. It had also been turned down to secure it." He shook his head. "That doesn't make sense. I can understand someone wanting to keep the stall door closed..."

Evie finished the sentence for him by thinking

someone had wanted to make sure George Stevens wouldn't come out.

Frowning, Evie stood on her tiptoes and looked into the stall. "Can you lift the light a bit, please?"

"What is it?" Tom asked.

"There's no lantern in there. How did he find his way in?"

Tom nodded. "This is definitely suspicious and we need to let Sterling Wright know and contact the local constabulary."

Turning to look at the doctor, Evie wondered what would happen next. The doctor had only felt for a pulse. He hadn't inspected the body for wounds.

"I think you should go and talk to Sterling. Lotte and I will stay here." She heard Tom cross the cobblestoned yard. When the sound of his footsteps receded, she turned to the doctor. "What do you think happened to him?"

He dug inside his pocket and, retrieving a handkerchief, he wiped his glasses clean. "The police will want one of their own to look at the body."

"You must have some idea," Evie insisted.

"I'm afraid I don't."

Evie didn't understand his reluctance.

Lotte nudged her head toward the door suggesting she wanted a private word with her. Excusing herself, Evie followed Lotte outside.

"Could you distract him, please? Take him back inside and have him check on Caro. I want to go through George Stevens's pockets before the police arrive and I obviously can't do it with him there. He looks like a stickler for rules."

They moved quickly. Although the doctor took some convincing to leave his post.

Along the way, Evie asked, "Why was Caro unconscious for so long?"

"Her cheek felt tender," he said. "As I said, I suspect she received a blow to the face and that knocked her out cold."

Walking back inside, the place remained a hive of activity with the footmen rushing upstairs with trays of more food and glasses. Glancing toward the kitchen she saw the staff busy cleaning and wiping down surfaces. Evie hadn't kept track of the time. She'd been too busy observing everyone.

They found Caro sitting up and looking quite alert. Evie saw that as a good sign and the others appeared to be pleased and relieved with her recovery too. Her cheek still looked red and would, no doubt, change color soon.

"Toodles went back upstairs to keep an eye on everyone," Henrietta explained. "We thought it best to stay here."

Evie smiled at Caro. "How do you feel?"

Caro looked uncertain for a moment and Evie remembered she'd been playing the role of Lady Carolina Thwaites. "Cousin Carolina?" she prompted with a nod of encouragement. Whatever happened, she thought it would be a good idea to keep up the pretense.

"I'm feeling better, Cousin Evie. I've been trying to remember what happened." Caro brushed a hand across her brow. "I remember I'd been following someone. Even then, I couldn't tell if it was a man or a woman because they had a big coat on with the collar turned up and they wore some sort of hat."

"Did you get a sense of how tall they were?"

Caro gave a slight shake of her head and winced. "The person moved quickly and might have been slouching. Or maybe the coat was too heavy."

"Did you follow him down the back stairs?"

"Yes."

"And where did you initiate your chase?"

Caro bit the edge of her lip. "Downstairs." After a moment, she gave a firm nod. "Yes, downstairs. I remember going into the library." Caro winced again. "Wait a minute. That's when I heard a door opening but not in the library." She closed her eyes.

"Take your time," Evie encouraged.

"I heard someone walking by. I think it must have been a woman. I sensed a lightness to the footsteps and then I became confused because I heard another set of footsteps coming from the opposite direction. I suspected it might have been a secret assignation. Wanting to be sure, I edged toward the door and tried to peer through the gap but I took too much care in not making any noise so I got to the door just as the door opposite was being closed."

Two people meeting in secret could be explained, Evie thought. As Caro had said, it might have been a secret assignation. They had already seen Helena Lloyd breaking away from the hunt to meet someone and house parties were notorious playgrounds for people wishing to experience the thrill of a forbidden tryst.

Caro tapped her finger against her chin. "I can't explain why I have this feeling there might have been someone else in the room."

"A third person? Did you hear voices?"

Caro closed her eyes again. After a moment, she smiled. "I heard a chair scraping against the floor. It didn't make the sort of sound you'd expect when someone moves a chair. Rather... it sounded as though someone had bumped into it and that happened just as the other two who entered closed the door."

"Are you suggesting they might have been in a dark room?"

Caro nodded and, straightening, she gasped. "Moments later, I heard the door open again. I looked through the gap in the door in time to see someone disappear down the corridor. That's when I took a chance and followed but they moved with haste and I nearly lost them." She narrowed her eyes and spoke with care as if trying to keep track of her thoughts. "I went upstairs. Yes. I followed them up the stairs and caught up with them as they disappeared inside a room. Then a maid came along so I had to hide. I slipped inside a room and waited for the hallway to clear. I had my ear pressed to the door and as soon as I heard someone walk by, I peered out. The person wore the coat I mentioned. They must have gone into the room to get it."

"A man's coat or a woman's coat?"

Caro gave a firm nod. "A man's coat. It had broad shoulders."

Could a woman have tried to disguise herself in a man's coat?

"How did the person walk? With heavy steps or light steps?" Henrietta asked, her voice full of intrigue.

"I couldn't really say. I think I focused too much on the coat. I can't say for sure, but I think they might have been wearing men's shoes." Caro tilted her head. "Actually, I did notice they were big. I'd even say they were oversized."

"I suppose the person could have changed their shoes," Henrietta mused.

Evie swung away and began pacing. Two or possibly three people had met in a room opposite the library. Then one of them went upstairs, entered a room and emerged wearing a large coat.

Had Caro witnessed a meeting of conspirators and had they drawn straws?

Evie's imagination tried to tap into anything that might yield an idea worth pursuing. Despite not knowing how George Stevens had died, she had no trouble believing someone had killed him.

There were too many thoughts racing through her mind as well as ongoing concerns for Caro's wellbeing. It didn't surprise her when she spoke out loud, "We know the guests staying here are all involved in the racing world and have some sort of association with Sterling Wright."

Sara and Henrietta nodded.

"We also know…" Evie remembered she hadn't actually, told them about George Stevens. Turning, she looked toward the door to make sure no one else would overhear her. "We found a body in the stables."

Sara and Henrietta gasped while Caro's eyes widened.

"George Stevens."

"He's dead?" Sara asked. "That's why you came to fetch the doctor?"

"Yes. The doctor confirmed it."

"Do you suppose the person Caro saw went out there to kill George Stevens?" Henrietta asked.

"It sounds like a wild idea. Especially as we don't know what caused his death."

"But it's possible," Sara said.

Evie nodded. And, they either had a handful or a houseful of suspects.

When Caro closed her eyes again, Evie gasped. "Caro?"

"Oh, I'm still alive. I just wanted to retrace my steps to see if I missed anything."

"Try not to exert yourself. It will come back to you," Henrietta smiled. "Perhaps we can make ourselves useful and take notes."

"We?" Sara asked.

"Yes, I'm afraid I don't have my spectacles. In any case, your handwriting is more elegant than mine."

While Henrietta and Sara sorted out the writing implements, Evie sat with Caro and tried to sort through the information swimming around her head.

When the police arrived, she and the others would have to tell them everything they knew. Or rather, everything they had observed. That meant sticking to facts.

As a lady detective, she would want to be taken seriously. Everything she said would reflect her abilities.

"Now, we have what we need," Henrietta said as she sat down.

Sara rolled her eyes. "You mean, I have what I need to take notes."

"I have an excellent memory, so anything you miss I will be able to fill in later on." Henrietta smiled at Caro. "Would you like to start from the beginning?"

"So much for your excellent memory," Sara whispered.

CHAPTER 16

om walked into the butler's office and stopped at the door to look at Caro. His expression shifted from concerned to relieved. "The police are on their way."

"How did Sterling Wright take the news?" Evie asked.

"He remained calm. His butler read the situation and directed all the footmen to fill everyone's glasses. I'm not sure that was the best idea since the police will want to speak with all the guests. However, it's understandable for him to want to keep everyone calm. I followed Sterling into his study and that's when he looked at a loss. His butler had to come to the rescue and make the telephone call."

"How long ago did he make the call?"

"Five minutes."

Evie turned to the others. "We'll be back shortly." Taking Tom's arm, she led him out of the butler's room and waited until they were outside to say, "I brought the doctor in so Lotte could look through George Steven's pockets."

They hurried across the yard toward the stables and walked in just as Lotte was straightening. She turned and looked lost for words.

"What's happened?" Evie asked. "What did you find?"

Lotte held the lantern up and stretched her other hand out.

"Is that blood?"

Nodding, Lotte looked around for something to clean her hand with. "I checked his head. There's a wound in the back."

Something that could have been determined with a simple examination if only the doctor had committed to it. "Does it seem odd that the doctor did nothing more than check his pulse?"

Lotte shook her head. "I noticed something odd about him. When he kneeled down, he hesitated. I think he recognized Gory George Stevens."

"I keep forgetting he has, or rather, he *had* a reputation."

"I suspect the doctor wanted to minimize his involvement," Lotte suggested.

"Surely you're not saying he fears some sort of retaliation from George's criminal cronies."

"It's possible."

They heard the sound of sirens approaching.

A sense of urgency swept through Evie. "We only have a few minutes. A part of me thinks we should just step away. But we already know something really bad happened here. How did he get that head wound?"

One by one, they turned toward the stall.

Evie shuddered. "I'd hate to think Mighty Warrior had anything to do with this. Since there's a head wound, we have to assume there is a weapon. The killer must have taken it with him." She glanced around. "Or used something and replaced it." Even with the limited light, she could see a variety of tools in the stables that could be used as a deadly weapon.

"The stall had been securely locked," Tom reminded her.

Evie found that most puzzling. "Someone could have hit him over the head and then locked the stall door."

"Why?" Lotte asked. "To make it look like an accident?"

"To blame the horse. That would be my guess." Picking up the spare lantern, Evie edged toward the stall. "Let's try to be thorough. This might be our only chance before the police arrive."

Limited by what they could see under the light from the lantern and without actually going inside the stall, they tried to cover every corner they could see with the naked eye.

Evie gasped. "There. I think I see something in the middle of the stall." Mighty Warrior hadn't moved from the corner and he still looked slightly agitated.

"I see it," Lotte said. "It looks like broken glass. They might be his spectacles." She looked over her shoulder at the body and confirmed it. "I didn't actually notice them missing until now. Wait… I see something else."

"Yes, I see it too, but what is it?" Evie held the lantern as far as she could.

"I'm not sure but it looks like a syringe," Tom said.

The sound of motor cars coming to a stop had them all stepping back. A conversation ensued. Evie imagined

Sterling Wright had met the constables outside. Moments later, the stable door opened.

A police officer in a suit walked in and, removing his hat, he took in the scene. "I'm Detective Inspector Evans. Would you all step outside, please. An officer will take your names."

All three moved without questioning the detective's request. Although, in Evie's opinion, he should have asked a few basic questions to establish their reasons for being there as well as for the sake of expediency since they might have seen something of value.

Outside, there were two constables holding up lanterns. Another one greeted them. He had a small notebook in hand and a pencil ready to take their names.

Providing their details without argument, they then headed back inside only to stop when a voice boomed across the yard.

"Wait a moment."

They all turned and saw the detective signaling for them to return.

Before they reached him, he had a brief word with the constable and Evie imagined he asked him for their names.

"Lady Woodridge," the detective said before identifying the others.

Evie thought he looked too young to be a detective. Especially one in charge of a possible murder investigation. He had a clean-shaven face. His clothes were neatly pressed. In fact, she saw no sign of having hurried to put himself together. Even his shoes were spotless and shiny.

This man, Evie thought, liked to take care of details.

"I'd like to know what you were all doing out here."

He looked at all three of them. Evie waited for him to rest his attention on Tom, but he didn't. Instead, he continued to look at each of them.

That struck her as unusual. In her experience, men tended to direct their serious questions to men.

When the others didn't answer straightaway, Evie said, "Our friend, Caro, suffered an injury earlier. Someone struck her. We wanted to see if we could find anything to lead us to the identity of her attacker."

The detective slipped his hands inside his pockets. "Is that when you contacted the local constabulary?"

Evie glanced at the others. "We were consumed with concern for Caro." And, she thought, they had been more preoccupied with instigating their own search.

He gestured with his head toward the stables. "Do you know the man's identity?"

Lotte adjusted her monocle. "Gory George Stevens."

"I assume you found him."

They all nodded.

The detective continued to study them.

The constables holding the lanterns stood beside them so Evie assumed the detective had no trouble reading their expressions.

Leaning slightly forward, he asked, "Were you surprised to find him?"

Evie spoke up. "Yes, indeed. We were."

The detective crossed his arms. "Lady Woodridge, you seem to be very well composed." He turned to Lotte. "As are you, Miss Woodridge."

It took Evie a moment to remember Lotte had disguised herself as her cousin Ophelia Woodridge and had provided the constable with that name. She remained in character and had somehow managed to keep the monocle in place. How would she explain herself if questioned further? Did she have a right as a lady detective to safeguard her identity while working a case?

Lotte raised her chin. "Lady Woodridge and I have seen worse. During the war, Lady Woodridge made Halton House available as a convalescent home for injured soldiers."

"You mean, for injured *officers*," the detective corrected.

Not seeing the point to his remark, Evie said, "As a matter of fact, no. While other houses were set up specifically for officers, we made a point of welcoming soldiers. Many of our local men were injured and we felt it only right that they should recover close to home. I am personally not immune to the shock of seeing a dead body, but as my cousin pointed out, I have seen worse."

"Yes, I see. However, that was during the war. This is a social occasion. I assume you were not expecting to find a dead body in the stables."

Evie shivered. "Perhaps my response has been stymied by the weather. It is rather cold out here."

"And that's what also puzzles me, my lady. I would have expected someone of your stature to send someone else out here to investigate."

"I was upset by Caro's injury and couldn't just sit about doing nothing."

"I see."

Did he really? Evie wondered how long it would take for the detective to warn her off and what tone he would employ to do so. Her name had already been linked to one major criminal case. It would be naïve to think the detective had not read about it.

He turned to Lotte. "Miss Ophelia Woodridge."

Lotte adjusted her monocle.

"Or is it Lotte Mannering? You bear a striking resemblance to the lady detective."

"Pardon?" Lotte asked.

The edge of his lip lifted. "Yes, the jig is up. Now, would you all mind telling me what you were doing here?"

In the spirit of co-operation and transparency, Evie wanted to tell the detective everything. But where would she start? "Detective, this is a crime scene and we don't wish to take up any of your valuable time. However, we were expecting some sort of trouble. Just not something as grave as this or, indeed, as the assault on Caro."

They heard a motor car approaching. As it drew closer, Evie recognized it as another police vehicle. It came to a stop and a couple of men in suits jumped out followed by two more constables.

The detective excused himself and went to have a word with them. The new arrivals then went inside.

"I'm guessing they have been directed to deal with the guests," Lotte said.

The detective returned. "Now, where were we? Oh, yes. You were all about to share your insights."

Evie could not hide her surprise. The police did not normally accept outside interference in their investigations, nor did they invite it. In fact, they discouraged it.

He gestured toward the stables. "Follow me." He turned and led them back to the scene of the crime.

Evie leaned in and whispered, "How much are we telling him?"

Lotte shrugged. "Let him ask the questions."

"Are you suggesting we refrain from volunteering information?"

"I'm suggesting we play it by ear. He's already caught us by surprise once. I don't know about you, but I'm confused and that could work against us."

Evie agreed. "Yes, I'm having difficulty reading him. Perhaps he belongs to a new school of thought. How old do you think he is?"

"No older than thirty."

Shaking her head, Evie whispered, "I hope he's not trying to get us to incriminate ourselves. We should be very careful what we reveal to him."

"So much for the truth setting us free," Tom mused.

The detective stood aside to let them through. Inside the stables, a constable had taken care of lighting more lanterns.

"You will find a broken pair of spectacles in the stall," Lotte offered without preamble. "And what appears to be a syringe."

The detective looked at Evie.

Taking it as a prompt to speak, Evie cleared her throat. "We found him inside the stall and we felt we needed to determine if he needed assistance."

The detective's eyebrow cocked up.

"However," Evie continued, "we were concerned about the horse, Mighty Warrior. He looked agitated."

The detective turned to the constable. "See if there's a free stall. We'll have to move the horse. Get one of the stable hands to help you. And be careful what you step on. It could be evidence."

"That's very sensible. Why didn't we think of that?" Evie whispered. Frowning, she stepped back and looked outside. She could see several constables. Looking toward the house, she saw a couple of people standing by the window and assumed they were servants.

With all this commotion, Evie thought, why hadn't the stable hands come out to see what was happening? She assumed they slept nearby.

The detective fixed his attention on them again. "You were saying."

So far, Evie thought, they'd divulged the steps they'd taken. She assumed anyone else would have done the same. What else could they tell him?

"Do I need to prompt you with more specific questions?" he asked.

Evie nodded. "It would help."

"You said you came out here to see if you could find something or someone responsible for your friend's attack?"

"That's correct."

"Do you have any suspicions you'd like to share with me?"

Once again, they were all surprised by his question.

He seemed to notice this. "I ask because you have all clearly been here all evening. Did you notice any suspicious behavior? Perhaps someone missing from the gathering?"

Evie nodded. "One person has been missing all evening. Archie Arthurs. He's a guest here and is staying at the house. We haven't actually asked. For all we know, he decided he wouldn't attend the ball." Looking at Lotte, Evie encouraged her to fill in the rest.

Lotte shrugged. "You might as well know we are on a case."

"I see. And is this something you can share with me?"

Evie expected him to lose his patience but, instead, he appeared to be intent on getting as much information out of them as possible.

Lotte told him about the threatening letters.

"And you are all in disguise now?" he asked.

"Only me," Lotte said. "Mr. Winchester and Lady Woodridge have come as themselves. Oh, there's also Lady Carolina Thwaites. She's actually Lady Woodridge's maid."

His gaze slid over to Evie. He looked at her for a long moment. "Your lady's maid is disguised as..."

"My cousin, thrice removed. She's played that role several times to great acclaim. At least, from those in the know."

"And what, precisely, did you hope to accomplish?"

"We only wanted to observe." Evie bit the edge of her lip to stop herself from saying more. If Henrietta had been there, Evie knew without a single doubt she would have divulged everything they knew, including the fact they had engaged the services of Mrs. Green and had witnessed a possible affair in the making. Evie found herself smiling because Henrietta would not have left a single detail out. Indeed, she would have made a point of mentioning the donkey and cart.

Digging inside his pocket, the detective produced a small leather-bound notebook. "These threatening letters you mentioned, do they contain some sort of demand?"

They all shook their heads.

"Not in any detail. However," Lotte said, "we think Marjorie Devon has been asked to do something."

"Such as?"

Evie interjected, "Detective, this is all supposition on our part."

"I'd like to hear it."

"If I may," Tom said.

"By all means," the detective invited.

"We know Gory George Stevens wanted to purchase Mighty Warrior. We also know Sterling Wright didn't wish to sell the horse. We suspect the threatening letters have something to do with George Stevens' desire to get the horse back."

The detective tapped his pen against his notebook. "You think he used Marjorie Devon to influence a different outcome."

"Quite possibly."

Evie brushed her finger on her chin. "Yes, but where does that syringe fit in?"

"Indeed." The detective walked over to the stall.

As he leaned over and looked inside, Tom explained how they had found the stall door closed with the latch secured in place.

The detective surprised them for a third time by asking, "Do you think someone else closed it?"

They all shrugged.

"There might be a group of people involved," Evie revealed. "We observed several people missing from the ball."

The detective swung around. "When did that happen?"

After Evie explained how she had been dancing with

Tom and had been keeping her eye on everyone staying at Hillsboro Lodge, the detective asked for the names of those missing.

Evie did her best to remember. Turning to Lotte, she asked, "Did I miss anyone?"

"Archie Arthurs. You noticed him missing from the start."

The constable returned and had a private word with the detective who nodded.

"Has something happened?" Lotte asked.

To their utter astonishment, the detective shared the information. "The stable hands are all fast asleep. The constable has been unable to stir them awake. It appears they have been drugged."

CHAPTER 17

*T*he stable boys, drugged?

Had someone wanted to make sure George Stevens wouldn't be disturbed in the stables? Or... Had someone or a group of people made sure they wouldn't have any witnesses to the crime they'd planned on committing?

"Does this suggest someone planned to kill him?" Evie heard herself ask, only to say, "That is, if he was indeed killed."

"We will have to wait for the official verdict. However..." The detective looked over his shoulder. "There is a wound on the back of his head. It is about the size of a horseshoe."

"Surely... Surely you're not suggesting Mighty Warrior killed him." Even as she spoke, Evie knew it could be more than possible. She hurried to the horse's defense. "It would explain the syringe. The horse might have felt threatened." Frowning, Evie looked at Tom.

"Countess? Are you about to say he meant to kill the horse?"

"Sterling Wright said he wouldn't sell him Mighty Warrior. Consider this... If George Stevens couldn't have it, then no one else would have it."

"I think we should tell the detective the rest," Tom said.

"There's more?" the detective asked.

Mentioning the fact everyone who had gone missing had then returned to the ballroom only to disappear again, Evie finished by saying, "This sounds like a conspiracy." And, she thought, it could all somehow be linked to the threatening letters. "Before someone attacked Caro, she heard a couple of people going into a room. There might have been a third person."

They heard a motor vehicle stopping outside the stables.

"I think perhaps you should all return inside. That will be the ambulance, here to take the body away."

Halfway back to the house, Evie murmured, "Are either of you surprised by the detective's behavior?"

Lotte nodded. "I've never experienced anything like it. As you said, he must be a new breed of detective."

Tom smiled. "Either that or Evie's reputation has preceded her and he wants to tap into her insight."

Before entering the house, Evie drew the attention of one of the constables. "Please let the detective know we can be contacted at Halton House." Turning to the others, she said, "I don't see the point of remaining here any longer. Besides, I still believe Caro's life might be in peril. Someone might think she could identify them. I would like to take her home where she will be safe."

"Oh, thank goodness," they heard Henrietta exclaim.

She stood at the doorway, clearly looking out for them. "What has been going on? We didn't dare leave Cousin Carolina alone and no one will tell us anything."

"We've had an eventful night, Henrietta. I think it would be best to get out of everyone's way and let the police do their job."

"I see, you've been chastised."

"On the contrary." Turning to Lotte, Evie felt and sounded surprised when she said, "I actually feel we served a purpose." It would be interesting to see if the detective would call on them the next day. "Is Caro up to walking?"

Before Henrietta could say anything, Tom suggested bringing the motor car around. "I'll go tell Edmonds."

"But what about our unfinished business here?" Henrietta asked. "Surely there is more we can do."

Insisting they needed to leave, Evie said, "We'll only get in everyone's way, I'm sure."

"What if they lie? Shouldn't you wait to see if they do? I'm sure the detective will want the facts verified."

"We already told him everything we saw," Evie insisted. "As well as a few assumptions we've made."

Henrietta shuddered. "This will give me a restless night."

"I'm sorry, Henrietta. Perhaps a cup of hot cocoa will help you sleep."

"Just don't be surprised to find me at your doorstep early tomorrow morning."

"What's this?" Sara asked as she emerged from the butler's room.

Henrietta filled her in on the developments. "I feel like

a child being sent to bed before hearing the end of the story."

Lotte and Evie went upstairs to collect everyone's coats and were not surprised to see the guests gathered around the great hall. The music had stopped and they were all talking in hushed whispers.

One of the detectives had commandeered the library and, judging by the vibe of expectancy Evie picked up, everyone sat in readiness to be interviewed.

The butler called a footman to assist them with carrying their coats. As they waited, Evie glanced around and took note of all the people of interest they had been observing. "I don't see anyone fidgeting or complaining about being interviewed by the police."

"Do you think that's a sign of a guilty person?" Lotte asked. "I've been at this job for a while and there doesn't appear to be a specific trait. Some guilty people complain bitterly, while others bide their time and focus on portraying themselves as innocent."

"And yet both could be guilty?" Evie asked.

Nodding, Lotte added, "They always slip up and do something to give themselves away."

"Or they leave a trail of evidence."

"Precisely, and it's a detective's job to find it and make sense of it."

So what information did they have so far? "Apart from the fact some people were absent from the ball, can we link anything else we have learned to George Stevens' death? Something that can be used as irrefutable proof?"

"Now you're beginning to sound like a lady detective."

Evie searched for Sterling Wright and his fiancée, but she couldn't see them anywhere. "I suppose Sterling will understand if we leave without saying goodnight. I wonder if anyone will question why we are not remaining."

When the footman had all their coats, he led the way and they went down the servants' stairs. To Evie's surprise, he didn't show any signs of finding the idea of them using the back stairs strange.

Belatedly, it occurred to ask Lotte, "Are you annoyed because I suggested we leave?"

"Not at all," Lotte said. "We've done enough for one night. Apart from continuing to do what we were doing, I don't really see the point of remaining." Nudging Evie, Lotte pointed to the footman. She cleared her throat, and said, "There's been quite a commotion here tonight."

He turned slightly. "I hope it hasn't ruined your evening, madam."

"Do you know anything about what happened?"

"There have been whispers about a body discovered in the stables."

"I can confirm it for you. We were the ones who found the body."

"Was it one of the guests?" he asked.

"Yes, indeed. You might have seen him. Mr. George Stevens." Lotte went on to describe him.

"Oh, yes. I believe I served him a drink this evening."

"Did you happen to notice anything unusual tonight? Anyone coming down this way?"

"Someone other than yourselves?" He shook his head. "No. I spent most of the evening in the ballroom. The others might know something."

Lowering her voice, Lotte said, "We would be very keen to hear about it."

"I believe arrangements could be made," he said just as they reached the ground floor and the butler's room at which point he proceeded to assist everyone into their coats.

While Lotte focused on negotiating with the footman, Evie walked up to Caro. "We are taking you home."

Sidling up to her, Henrietta murmured, "We will have to make arrangements. I'll explain in a moment."

Evie tried to read the dowager's raised eyebrow expression but she became confused when Henrietta signaled to the housekeeper.

"Mrs. Brook will be keeping us abreast of the situation."

"I see." She turned and saw Lotte still in deep conversation with the footman. All along, Henrietta had been busy expanding her web of information spies.

Thanking the housekeeper and maid, they made their way to the waiting motor cars. The ambulance had left but the police vehicles were still there.

As Henrietta climbed into the motor, she turned to Evie, "I'm afraid I have committed to compensating the housekeeper for her troubles. It seems information will not be freely given. I'm sorry, I fear I have failed the team. This will cost you."

"I see. It's coming out of my pocket." Evie smiled.

"I'm sure it will be worth it since we'll be receiving information, more or less, straight from the horse's mouth." Henrietta sat back and sighed. After a moment, she turned to Evie and smiled. "Race you back to Halton House?"

$\approx$

Later that night
The library, Halton House

Seeing Evie entering the library, Tom asked, "Has everyone been tucked in for the night?"

"Yes, Henrietta grumbled about spending the night here. She actually said she would feel safer in the dower house since we would most likely be targets."

"What about Caro?"

Evie stopped to pour two glasses of brandy. Frowning, she turned to Tom. "Did you say you don't like brandy or was that an excuse to avoid spending half an hour in the company of the other men?"

He grinned.

Taking the drink over to him, she sat down. "Caro talked about having my hair shingled and going through my wardrobe because she thought the color scheme needed to be refreshed. If I didn't know her at all, I would have suspected her of rambling and not being quite right in the head. However, her chatter remained the same as always. I asked Millicent to sit with her. I left her reading *The Secret Garden* but couldn't help noticing she had a copy of D.H. Lawrence's *Sons and Lovers* tucked out of sight, or so she thought. When I came out of Caro's room, I found Edmonds had settled down for the night in a comfortable chair by the door. Apparently, he is determined to keep watch."

Tom told her he had made the rounds of the house and the grounds and had spoken with the stable hands who had all been alerted of the night's events. "I doubt anyone will get much sleep tonight."

"I can't imagine anyone breaking into the house to harm Caro. She could not have seen anything. You saw how dark it was outside."

"True. However, I'm sure we're dealing with a desperate person or persons willing to do anything."

"To what end? That's what I don't understand. What did they gain by George Stevens' death?"

They sat watching the fire and listening to the soothing crackling of the logs. The clock on the mantle struck the hour. One in the morning. If nothing had happened at the ball, they would only just be thinking about returning home.

"Halton House is like a fortress," she mused, almost as if she needed reassuring. Telling herself all would be well, she asked, "What were you reading?"

"The newspaper. What is the country to do with so many surplus women?"

"I wish they'd ease up and stop blaming women and saying they have become a burden on society. It's not their fault so many men did not return from the war. In fact, these women deserve empathy. Society places so many expectations on them and now, through no fault of their own, they are being denied the opportunity of marriage and, as a result, they have been turned into outcasts."

"I had no idea you held such strong opinions."

"If I didn't hold them, I should." Evie sighed into her glass. "I read the newspapers too and I try to ignore such articles but they are infuriating. I have no trouble imagining the average person going around and blaming the country's woes on women who are now destined to remain single."

"So you don't think it's a serious issue?"

"Actually, I do. One article suggested they should pack up their worldly goods and travel to Canada or Australia where, apparently, there are more men than women. Not only are they portrayed as burdens but they are also thought of as disposable. That is simply not right. Just because marriage might no longer be an option doesn't mean they can't lead productive lives." Evie lowered her gaze and smiled. "I've already been married once, perhaps I should send you on your way. It feels greedy to snatch another man."

"Do I get a say?"

Shifting, she finished her brandy and set the glass down. "Marjorie Devon might have been one of the two million surplus women. She lost her fiancée in the Great War but now she's managed to land herself another man."

Tom set his glass down and studied her. "Something tells me there's a thought taking shape in your mind."

"What would she do to maintain the status quo?"

Tom didn't need to give it much thought. "She could make herself out to be a victim. Gain sympathy. Tap into a man's protective instincts."

That would make her terribly cunning, Evie thought.

"Do you think Marjorie Devon is capable of writing the letters to herself?"

Evie laughed. "Wouldn't that be funny. No one would dare believe it."

Tom tipped his head back. "She knew about the letters and yet the knowledge her life might be in danger didn't stop her from getting out and about."

Evie nodded. "Because she knew the threat had been fabricated. It's an interesting theory. Unfortunately, it would mean the letters have no connection to George Stevens' death." Stretching, she yawned. "So much for distractions."

"So you're not serious about the idea of Marjorie inventing the threat?"

"She's young and pretty and Sterling Wright seems to care for her. She'd have to be supremely insecure to feel she stood on shaky ground with him."

"What happened to thinking George Stevens had sent her the letters?"

Evie chortled. "He's… he was a criminal. Do you really think he'd resort to writing letters to get his message across? If he'd wanted to deliver a message, he would have sent a crony to do it in a threatening way."

"Are you now saying she has no connection to his death?"

"I think we were distracted by the letters. Maybe if we stop thinking about them, we might find another trail to follow. I wonder how the police will tackle the case."

"They might not see any reason to investigate it," Tom suggested.

"Because of his criminal life? Surely everyone deserves justice."

"Your impartiality is commendable."

Evie grinned. "Did you fall for it?"

Tom grinned right back at her. "Did you?"

They spent another hour trying to sift through what they knew only to hit another dead end.

They followed their conversation with a quiet study of the various newspapers stacked on the shelves.

"Here's another article about Sterling's purchase of the horse." Tom handed her the newspaper.

"Oh, there's a photograph of the horse."

"Yes, and a description."

"Chestnut with a white diamond shape. I remember Sterling describing him as brown."

"And you found that odd."

Evie shrugged. "Most people I know who are enthusiastic horse owners are so passionate about their horses they always talk at great length about them." Despite the warmth from the fire, Evie shivered. "I expect the detective will be paying us a visit tomorrow. He will most likely wish to speak with Caro. The moment I stop thinking, my mind fills with images of something really dreadful happening to Caro. I hold myself responsible. She should not have gone out by herself."

"Caro has her own mind."

"Yes, and I'm usually at the receiving end of her thoughts." Inspecting her nails, she hummed. "The more involved I become in this venture, the more she will want to participate. What if it happens again? I'm not sure I can accept the burden of responsibility."

"We will have to be more organized and safety conscious," Tom assured her.

"I'm surprised you didn't say there is danger in crossing the road."

"I didn't feel I needed to remind you."

"I wonder… What if I find her a husband?"

Tom laughed. "You want to domesticate her?"

"It's worth a try. At least she won't come to harm because of me."

"Do you actually believe Caro would settle for marriage when she could have a life of adventure?"

"She might. I'll just have to make sure she has the option to choose." She glanced at him. "I believe I just sounded like Henrietta."

CHAPTER 18

The next day

*E*vie reached over her head to pull the bell only to remember she had told Caro to take a couple of days to recuperate.

Someone, probably Millicent, had drawn the curtains so she couldn't tell how early or late she had woken up.

Closing her eyes for a moment, she tried to remember if she and Tom had made any plans for the day. The night before, they had covered a lot of ground without getting anywhere. As far as they were concerned, the matter now rested fully in the hands of the police. They alone would decide if and how to proceed.

Flinging the bedcovers off, she jumped to her feet and drew the curtains open. "It's definitely morning. And, judging by the mist, quite early."

Half an hour later, she stood in front of her wardrobe

wondering how Caro always managed to chat while selecting one piece of clothing after the other, all matched perfectly.

She looked over her shoulder and cringed at the pile of clothes she had brought out. "There is definitely no such thing as a simple task."

Picking up a skirt, she set it to one side. "Who left the ballroom first?" She pointed to the skirt. "Marjorie?" Next, she picked up a blouse and set it beside the skirt. "At the same time, we noticed George Stevens and his wife were no longer in the ballroom." Unfortunately, she thought, no one had thought to follow George Stevens. Selecting another blouse, she placed it next to Marjorie's skirt. "According to Caro, Lotte followed Marjorie at a discreet distance."

Walking back to the wardrobe, she removed three skirts and set them down alongside each other. "Henrietta and Sara followed the Prentiss couple, but they lost them…"

A light knock at the door had her swinging around.

Millicent walked in. Evie had no need for two lady's maids but after a brief visit from the town house, Millicent had fallen well and truly in love with Edgar and Evie hadn't had the heart to break the couple apart. Especially as, at the time, she had been intent on keeping her butler happy for fear that he might find another job and leave her.

Smiling, Millicent gave her a cheerful greeting and proceeded to chat as she put all the garments away.

"Milady, you didn't ring for me so I thought I would come up and see if you were awake."

Seeing her display of suspects dismantled, Evie gasped.

"Caro slept like a log but she's already dressed and insisting she will have breakfast downstairs with the rest of us and she will not listen to reason. So I had to rush here because she'd already started heading this way. I wouldn't be surprised if she has her ear pressed to the door, milady. She told me you will most likely trek out today and you should wear your warm boots with the fur lining and I should match it with your green tweed, the one with the hints of orange, not the one with the blue because she warned me you wore that a couple of days ago and if I don't heed her advice she is going to do dreadful things to me. I don't wish to test her."

Evie tried to follow Millicent's chatter but, as usual, she got lost along the way.

When Millicent stepped back, Evie realized she was dressed in the skirt she had used as a prop for Marjorie and a blouse she had used to identify George Stevens or had it been Lotte?

"I'm not sure about that blouse because it has the little mother of pearl buttons and I think this is the one Caro told me you shouldn't wear with this tweed, but I think it looks lovely so we'll keep it on and if Caro puts her foot down you might want to say you like it too, although, Caro is likely to tell you I have been a bad influence and you should not listen to me because I have no sense whatsoever."

"I promise." As she looked at her reflection, Evie asked, "How is Caro's cheek? Has it changed color?"

"It's quite sore, milady. While she hasn't complained, I did notice her wince a couple of times. The redness has faded and there are hints of blue and yellow and a touch of green. If anyone says someone slapped Caro they would be wrong because I grew up with three brothers and I know what a bruise looks like. Especially a bruise from a fist. Someone punched our Caro and she can't confirm it because she doesn't have a clear recollection of what happened last night so I suppose we will never know for sure. If only the person had worn a ring. Of course, that would have caused more damage but at least we would have some sort of lead to follow."

As Millicent talked, Evie found herself wondering if she actually breathed.

"Now, where is the hat Caro said you should wear today? I have a feeling you will be going out so I should have one ready for you. I know she has a system in place here and I don't want to disrupt it. Although, if you ask me, I would put all the light-colored clothes on the right and the darker shades on the left. That would make selecting them a lot easier."

"I would suggest it but, as you said, Caro has a system and I don't dare disrupt it."

"Maybe if she plays a bigger role in your investigations, I will step in and do her job. That way, I could introduce my system which, of course, she will reorganize at the first opportunity but I could always rearranged things again and soon enough she will tire of changing things back."

"That sounds like a solid plan, Millicent. Now, I think I'm all set to face the day. Thank you. I'll make sure to tell Caro you did a splendid job."

"Oh, you mustn't do that, milady. She'll think you're being critical of her work and, after what happened last night, we must be considerate of her sensibilities."

"Oh, if you say so."

"Of course, it wouldn't hurt to mention what a fine job I did."

Giving Millicent a reassuring smile, Evie made her escape. Along the way, she bumped into Tom.

"Where's the fire?" he asked.

"I believe I'm about to be introduced to a new routine. In any case, I'm in a bit of a daze. If I sound slightly distracted at breakfast, just click your fingers. Hopefully, I'll snap out of it."

Tom gave her a knowing smile. "Let me guess. Millicent looked after you this morning."

Evie nodded. "On the bright side, Caro appears to be on the mend. Oh, and I'm wearing a suspect."

"Pardon?"

"My skirt is Marjorie. Or is it my blouse? Heavens, never mind."

They walked down to the morning room and found Lotte already enjoying her breakfast.

"I see you have decided to continue on as my cousin, Ophelia," Evie observed as she studied Lotte's Bohemian looking blouse decorated with large blocks of orange and blue.

"I thought it would be easier, in case someone drops by unexpectedly."

Glancing at the selection of dishes on offer, Evie frowned. "Someone? Are you expecting someone from Hillsboro Lodge? Why would they come here?"

"You never know."

Looking toward the windows and the dismal looking day beyond, Evie said, "The only visitors we're likely to get are Henrietta and Sara but they spent the night here."

A footman standing nearby shook his head. "Begging

your pardon, my lady. Lady Henrietta left late last night. She woke up Edmonds and told him to drive her and Lady Sara back to the dower house."

"Did she give a reason?"

"She said something about needing to speak with her spy."

Evie huffed out a breath. She couldn't believe Henrietta had woken Edmonds up. Worse, she had put herself and Sara in possible danger.

Taking her place at the table, she tried to shake off her frustration.

"I'm willing to bet the detective will come by this morning," Tom offered as he sat down to enjoy his bacon and eggs."

"I do hope he telephones before he comes. Surely a man in his position can't afford to waste time. Caro might not be up to it. According to Millicent, Caro hasn't been able to recall anything new. If she had remembered something of significance, she would have informed us."

"You actually sound concerned by the prospect of a visit from the detective," Lotte said.

Evie felt unprepared to deal with the detective. "If you must know, he still puzzles me. I can't make heads or tails of his behavior." Drawing in a deep breath, she tried to distract herself with her breakfast but found her thoughts fixated on Henrietta's middle of the night exodus. Discreetly, she rubbed her fingers along the thumping pulse on her temple.

Edgar walked in and cast his critical eye over the trays of food. Satisfied with what he saw, he took his place in a corner.

"Good morning, Edgar."

Her butler inclined his head and greeted everyone.

Evie didn't see the point of asking if anyone had telephoned, but knowing Caro had taken her breakfast with everyone else downstairs, she asked, "How did you find Caro this morning?"

"My lady, I hope you don't think I am speaking out of turn, but I fear I am not at all pleased about Caro taking such risks."

"In other words, you disapprove." A wave of relief swept through her. Feeling the tension that had built around her shoulders ease away, Evie jumped at the opportunity to lighten the moment. "What if I told you I am about to officially become a lady detective?"

Edgar paled. "My lady? Surely you jest."

"Surely not. I wouldn't do that to you, Edgar. Perhaps under different circumstances, but not today."

Staring straight ahead, he gave it some thought. "I would be inclined to worry about the risks involved and perhaps even disapprove. However, since it's not my place to hold such opinions, I would offer all the support I could to ensure you succeed in your venture."

"You would?"

Edgar swallowed. "Most likely. Yes... Yes, I'm sure I would."

Evie smiled. "But will you?"

"Countess, you are torturing Edgar."

Evie gave Tom a brisk smile. "I think Edgar is worried I'll enlist Millicent's assistance."

Edgar groaned and swayed slightly.

Tom leaned in and whispered, "Are you mad? You know Edgar is likely to pack up and leave and take Millicent with him. What's come over you?"

"Oh, very well," Evie whispered. "Edgar, I do hope you realize I'm only teasing."

"Of course, it's perfectly understandable, my lady. In any case, I doubt Millicent would be of any help. She has many fine qualities but acting is not one of them. If ever you are in desperate need of her assistance, I will have to give her some helpful instructions."

That took Evie by surprise and made her wonder if Edgar had actually felt left out. "That's very generous of you, Edgar. Thank you." However, Evie couldn't help feeling she had been put on notice. In future, she would need to tread with care when enlisting the assistance of any of the servants. When Tom nudged her, she felt compelled to add, "I promise I will try to discourage Millicent from participating in our investigations."

"That would be much appreciated, my lady." Edgar cleared his throat. "However, it would also be totally unnecessary as we would all be only too happy to assist in any way we can."

Evie smiled brightly. "I knew you'd come around."

Tom nearly choked on his coffee. "Are you keeping track of the number of associates you're acquiring?"

"I consider myself quite fortunate to be surrounded by wonderfully helpful people." Turning to Lotte, Evie changed the subject and asked, "Do you think Sterling Wright will retain your services now that George Stevens is dead? I'm assuming he had a hand in writing the letters. Even if he didn't strike me as the type to put anything in writing."

"I have no idea. Assuming Sterling Wright didn't recognize me last night, he probably expects me to be staying at the cottage. Perhaps he's tried to contact me there."

The clock on the mantle struck the hour and they all looked up.

"It's almost as if we are all waiting for something to happen," Tom said. "Again."

Moments later, the door opened and a footman entered. He relayed a message to Edgar who then made the announcement.

"Detective Inspector Evans, my lady. He is waiting in the library."

Dabbing the edge of her lip with a serviette, Evie braced herself for the encounter while Tom surged to his feet and drew Evie's chair back.

"He might not wish to see us all," Lotte said, "but it might be a good idea for me to hover nearby."

"Yes, please. I have no idea what to expect from him and that worries me."

"Would you prefer a more predictable detective?" Tom asked.

"Yes, that would be comforting. But I believe you are about to tell me a predictable detective would warn me to steer clear of the investigation. Then again, he wouldn't have the opportunity because I have been nothing but an innocent bystander." Evie glanced at Tom.

Adjusting his tie, he smiled at Evie. "Are you trying to convince me or yourself?" Before she could answer, he added, "Of course, I support your version of the truth."

"I see it as a simple statement of fact. I agreed to join Lotte's efforts to uncover the author of a series of threatening letters. The rest is circumstantial."

The detective had come alone. He'd matched his dark gray suit with a royal blue tie. It seemed he made a habit of taking care of his appearance. In the daylight, he looked no older than thirty. His meticulous attention to detail included a pristine white handkerchief tucked into his breast pocket with such precision, Evie suspected he had used a ruler.

"Lady Woodridge, my apologies for bursting in on you unannounced."

"Good morning, Inspector Evans. We were actually hoping you'd come." Evie willed him to spill the beans and share all the information he had gathered. If only she had the power to influence him, she thought. She gestured to a group of chairs by the fireplace.

As Evie sat down, Tom went to stand by the fireplace and the detective sat opposite her.

"I wanted to ask your permission to speak with Lady Carolina Thwaites," he said.

Evie didn't need to look at Tom to know his eyebrows had hitched up just as hers had.

The detective gave her a small smile which he partly hid when he looked down at his shiny shoes. "I assume you wish to keep up with the pretense."

"It would simplify matters. Otherwise, I fear I might have some explaining to do to Sterling Wright. I did, after all, introduce Caro as my cousin."

His smile widened. "Thrice removed. Yes, thank you for sharing that with me."

Understanding dawned. She had provided the detective with a night's worth of entertainment. That, Evie knew, wouldn't be the first time.

"In any case, you don't need my permission to speak with… Cousin Carolina." She turned and found Edgar at the door. "Edgar, could you please send for Lady Carolina?"

The edge of his lip twitched. "And if I cannot locate Lady Carolina? Should I presume your lady's maid can find her?"

Out of the corner of her eye, she saw Tom's chest rise up and down in quick succession as if he could barely contain his laughter. "I'm sure someone knows where Lady Carolina can be found. Thank you, Edgar."

Edgar's eyes brimmed with amusement when he bowed his head and left the room.

"This is a very interesting household, my lady."

"Really? I hadn't noticed." Shifting to the edge of her chair, she said, "I suppose you'll want to speak to… my cousin in private."

"Not at all. Feel free to stay. This is not an interrogation. I'm only after whatever she might have remembered."

"Have there been any new developments?" she asked not really expecting him to answer.

"As a matter of fact, yes. We now have confirmation the syringe contained a toxic substance, strong enough to kill."

"Poison?"

He nodded.

"Is it safe to assume George Stevens meant to use it on Mighty Warrior?"

"It's the only explanation we can come up with," he said.

"Does he have any associates you can question?" Evie asked even as she realized she might be pushing her luck.

"It will take some work to fish them out." Frowning, he

asked, "Did you happen to hear anything at the ball about George Stevens and the host, Sterling Wright?"

Evie glanced over at Tom. "We only know what Sterling Wright told us. Considering how much George Stevens wanted to buy the horse back, it's difficult to understand why he would try to kill Mighty Warrior. Unless he realized he wouldn't get his way and if he couldn't have the horse, no one else could."

The detective studied her for a moment. "I can see why Inspector O'Neill holds you in high regard."

"I see. You have been in contact with him."

"He's been my mentor for a number of years. In fact, he is responsible for guiding me toward this profession."

The door to the library opened and Caro walked in dressed as Lady Carolina Thwaites.

The detective jumped to his feet. He took several deep swallows and after a lengthy moment, he said, "Thank you for making time for me, Lady Carolina."

Evie saw Caro's gaze slide over to her and would have sworn Caro offered a silent apology for the ruse. It surprised Evie. From the start, Caro had been only too happy to play the role and had appeared to be quite comfortable in it.

"I would have spoken with you last night," the detective continued, "but, under the circumstances, I thought it would be best to wait, at least until today. If you need more time…"

"No, I'll do my best to help." Caro took the chair next to Evie and related everything she could remember. "I'm afraid I still can't say if the person I followed was a man or a woman. In any case, I lost sight of them."

"Is that when you found yourself outside?" he asked, his voice gentling with each word.

Caro nodded.

"How long do you think you were there for?"

"I couldn't really say. We were all so fixated with keeping track of everyone. I'm sure I must have looked at a clock along the way, but I simply can't bring the image to mind." Caro looked up, her brows furrowing. She looked quite puzzled and then she brightened. "Now that I think about it, I stood outside and I didn't feel cold, but I'm usually quick to feel it. So it couldn't have been that long. Perhaps five minutes."

The detective took out his notebook and made a note.

Caro worried the edge of her lip. "I think I must have noticed the cold and decided to turn back and go inside. The way my mind works, I probably thought I could stand by a window and look out." Her eyes widened. "Yes, as I turned away, I heard someone approaching. They walked with determination and... that's when it happened. They knocked me out cold."

"It sounds as if you definitely got in someone's way," he said. "You are a remarkable woman for even attempting such a task."

Caro gave him a bright smile.

Evie's gaze bounced between them. They were both taking deep swallows and just looking at each other. The moment stretched to the point that Evie felt like an intruder.

Caro brushed her fingers along her cheek. "I remember waking up and feeling dazed."

"That's perfectly understandable. It must have been

quite a blow." The detective winced. "Do you think it felt like a small fist or a large fist?"

"It felt... solid and determined."

Evie wondered if a woman would be so confident as to deliver a solid blow. Perhaps if they thought they had a lot to lose by being recognized. She'd met many women determined enough to get what they wanted but she'd never seen one being physically violent.

Evie curled her fingers into the palm of her hand.

Could she throw a punch?

She certainly knew how to do it. Her male cousins had shown her and Tom had given her some instructions. Yes, she believed herself capable of it. In fact, if she came face to face with the person who had punched Caro, Evie knew she would not hesitate to serve a solid, reciprocal punch. It would be justified.

Saying he didn't wish to overexert Caro, the detective thanked them for their time, told them he would most likely be in touch again and excused himself and left.

CHAPTER 19

Thrills and spills

The library
Halton House

"I think I disappointed him," Caro said, her voice soft and pensive.

"Nonsense," Evie assured her. "You told him what you knew." Unfortunately, the detective had left before she and Tom could ask more questions about the investigation.

"He sounds… nice. Don't you think he sounds nice?" Caro asked.

"He does."

"And... he dresses well. I mean... he doesn't look scruffy." Caro nodded. "He has a gentle voice."

Evie glanced at Tom. "Yes, he has an interesting approach to his questioning."

Caro continued to look pensive. "I wonder how effective the tactic is with criminals."

"I doubt he uses the same tone with them," Evie whispered.

"Do you think he's harsh? I can't imagine him being harsh."

"I wouldn't worry about that, Caro. How are you feeling this morning?"

"Colorful. My bruise started changing color. Oh, heavens. Do you think he noticed? Of course, he did, but he was too polite to look directly at my bruise." After a moment of silent introspection, Caro jumped to her feet. "I should go check on Millicent. Who knows what she's doing to your wardrobe."

Evie watched her leave and found herself gaping.

"Interesting," Tom mused.

"Yes, interesting." Evie looked up at Tom. "I wonder, are we finding the same thing interesting?"

He gave a small nod. "The moment Caro walked in, the detective's tone softened, then he only had eyes for Caro."

Evie nodded. "I can't remember the last time I felt invisible."

Tom agreed. "Me too."

"We'll have to find out everything we can about the detective."

Tom laughed. "Seriously? Are you playing matchmaker? I mean... There's nothing wrong with that."

"You saw what I saw and it happened right in the

middle of an investigation. I think this is what's referred to as a blessing in disguise. It would help to know his first name. However…" Evie was interrupted by the door opening and Henrietta and Sara walking in.

"What's happened?" Henrietta demanded. "You both look perplexed."

Forgetting her earlier frustration with Henrietta for leaving in the middle of the night, Evie nodded. "Yes, we are rather pleasantly surprised. We believe Caro has acquired an admirer."

"You mean, Cousin Carolina."

"Both. The detective knows her real identity but was happy to go along with her ruse."

Henrietta hummed. "Considering the current state of affairs, with so many women destined to remain single, we must do everything in our power to encourage them. However, I have other pressing matters which require our immediate attention."

Sara settled down opposite Evie. "Henrietta couldn't wait to come and tell you in person. She has spent the morning working herself up into a frenzy."

"I suppose you noticed our absence at breakfast," Henrietta said as she sat down beside Sara. "I should apologize. I tossed and turned for half an hour and, unable to settle down, I…"

"You dragged me out of bed and forced me to go back to the dower house with you," Sara complained.

"All for a good cause. Although, as it turns out, it was actually a lost cause. My spy network has been shattered."

"How did that happen?" Evie asked.

"I'm afraid Hillsboro Lodge is beyond my people's reach."

"Oh, that's disappointing."

"It most certainly is. We must find a way to overcome the problem of a tightknit household." She glanced at the footman. "At least the housekeeper has agreed to share any news with us. Have you made the arrangements? Last night you agreed to pay her for information."

"My apologies, Henrietta. It slipped my mind. Perhaps we can send Edmonds over to Hillsboro Lodge." Evie gave it some thought. "Oh, I know. We could ask Mrs. Horace to prepare a thank you basket for looking after Caro. Edmonds can slip the payment in."

Henrietta tapped her umbrella on the carpet. "How soon can you organize it?"

"Straightaway," Evie assured her.

When Evie didn't make a move, Henrietta's eyebrows shot up. "How soon is straightaway?"

Sara smiled. "I told you she's in a state of frenzy."

Evie got up. When she turned toward the fireplace and the bell pull, Henrietta moaned softly.

"Henrietta, would you like me to go down to the kitchen and speak with Mrs. Horace myself?" Evie asked.

"That would be more expedient, Evangeline."

Leaning in, Tom whispered, "You're fighting a losing battle, Countess. I'll accompany you down."

"Only because you're afraid of what Henrietta will make you do if you remain," Evie whispered back.

They both headed for the door as Henrietta said, "That took some effort."

Tom managed to contain his laughter until they reached the door to the back stairs.

"Honestly, I don't know what's come over Henrietta."

"At least she's no longer twitching," Tom said.

"True."

Halfway down the stairs, they encountered Edgar coming up.

"My lady… I was just coming up to bring you a message."

Heavens, what now?

It had to be important for Edgar to come himself instead of sending a footman.

Edgar looked flustered and out of breath. "T-the… the housekeeper."

"Mrs. Horace?"

He shook his head and, still sounding out of breath, said, "No, the other housekeeper, Mrs. Brook. She's here."

Mrs. Brook?

Tom chortled. "The Hillsboro Lodge housekeeper came to us. Henrietta will be pleased."

They hurried down to the kitchen and found Mrs. Brook sitting down with Halton House's housekeeper, Mrs. Horace.

"She must know something really important," Evie whispered. "Do you carry money with you?"

Tom dug inside his pocket and drew out some bills.

Evie looked at them and took one. "How much are we supposed to give her? I didn't ask…" Taking another one, she added, "We should play it safe."

Tom gave her another one. "She might want to vacation in the Riviera."

They greeted Sterling Wright's housekeeper. "We were just about to set out to Hillsboro Lodge," Evie said. "Has something happened?"

Mrs. Brook looked at the money Evie held and smiled. "Yes, indeed. I thought I'd come and tell you myself."

Evie didn't know if she should pay her now or wait to hear the news. She had no idea how these transactions were supposed to be performed. Although, it made sense to withhold payment until she could be certain of the quality of the information.

Mrs. Brook gave her a knowing smile. "The police found something in the stables."

Evie called on her patience. It seemed Mrs. Brook wished to draw out the suspense.

She continued, "One of the stable boys saw them." The housekeeper held two fingers out and spread them slightly as if to indicate a distance or a measurement. "A small piece of fabric."

"What color?" Tom asked.

Mrs. Brook smiled. "Pink."

~

Moments later
The library

Marjorie Devon had worn a pink dress.

Why hadn't the detective shared the information?

Tom and Evie walked into the library and found Lotte sitting with Henrietta and Sara sipping tea.

"It's all been taken care of," Evie assured Henrietta. "Our timing could not have been better. The housekeeper came to us."

Henrietta set her teacup down. "Oh, thank heavens. A woman of action."

"A woman intent on getting her payment," Tom whispered.

"Worth every penny since she brought us some interesting news. Actually, more than pennies, but never mind all that." Evie told them about the fabric found in the stables.

"From Marjorie Devon's dress?"

"Yes. Most likely. Well, we can't think of anyone else who wore a pink dress last night." Evie imagined the detective had already discovered the link between the piece of fabric and the dress it had come from.

Had he questioned Marjorie?

Of course, he had.

The detective obviously knew how to do his job. The night before, they'd given him a list of names of people who had been absent at one time or another from the ballroom. If he hadn't thought of Marjorie as a suspect worth considering before, that piece of fabric must surely have put her at the top of his list now.

What had been her explanation?

Lotte stood up and walked to the window. "We now have proof Marjorie went to the stables. That's something."

"Yes," Evie said. "However, we don't know when she went there. Directly after she left the ballroom the first time? Or the second time. I wonder if we can make another connection? Thanks to Caro, we also know Marjorie had been fretting before George Stevens' arrival."

"Do you think she killed George Stevens?" Sara asked.

Evie nibbled the tip of her thumb. "The fabric puts her at the scene of the crime. That doesn't mean she had a hand in his demise. But she will have to explain herself." Evie glanced at Lotte. "And if the detective isn't convinced, he will look for motive." And, Evie thought, he would have the necessary resources.

Why hadn't the detective mentioned it? Had it been an oversight? Had he forgotten to tell them because he'd been dazzled by Caro? Of course, he was under no obligation to share news with them. Then again, he'd told them about the syringe.

Evie started pacing. She came full circle, looked up and saw Lotte had moved away from the window and had also started pacing around the room.

Stopping in front of Evie, Lotte asked, "What do you think?"

How could they put together the puzzle from a distance? "Maybe you should get in touch with Sterling Wright."

Lotte blinked. After a moment, she nodded.

Swinging around, they both resumed their pacing. Along the way, Evie glanced at Tom.

Henrietta groaned her displeasure. "Would someone please explain what is happening? You are all looking at each other. Is there some sort of secret language we are not privy to?"

Evie stopped and sat down in the nearest chair. "I'm trying to think of some questions."

"I have plenty of those," Henrietta said. "Would you like to hear some?"

Getting up again, Evie circled back and again met with Lotte who nodded and said, "I should go to Hillsboro Lodge now."

Evie nodded. As a seasoned detective, Lotte would

know how to wrangle information out of Sterling Wright. She could also justify her visit.

"Edgar," Henrietta hollered.

"My lady?"

"Oh, here you are. My apologies, I see you now. Do we have today's newspapers?"

"Certainly, my lady." Edgar directed a footman to fetch them.

Henrietta dug around her handbag. "Heavens, in my haste to come here I seem to have forgotten my spectacles."

When the footman brought the newspapers, Henrietta turned to Tom. "Could you please look through them to see if there is any mention of last night? And pull up a chair next to me. I want to make sure you don't miss anything."

Edgar provided the chair and Tom sat down, saying, "I promise I won't spare you the gory details."

Turning to Evie, Henrietta said, "Since you won't ask, I will volunteer a question. Had anyone considered the mysterious gentleman who arrived with the platinum blonde woman last night?"

Evie and Lotte stopped and looked at Tom.

"No, don't look at Tom. He is busy reading."

"Perhaps Lotte can find out his identity when she goes to Hillsboro Lodge," Evie suggested. "I must admit, I did not keep track of him."

"Well, he certainly looked suspicious."

"Yes, I mistook him for George Stevens. He had a certain look about him."

Tom set the newspaper down. "There is no mention of the death."

"Isn't that odd? George Stevens was a prominent member of the criminal world," Henrietta observed. "Doesn't the detective wish to get his name in print?"

"Evidently not."

The door to the library opened and Toodles walked in. "Here you all are. What did I miss?"

Sara grinned. "Cousin Carolina has an admirer."

Henrietta tapped her umbrella on the floor. "Could we please focus on one wedding at a time. I mean… On the murder."

Lotte headed for the door, saying, "I'm going to Hillsboro Lodge."

"As Cousin Ophelia or as yourself?" Evie asked.

That stopped Lotte in her tracks. "Good point. I'll have to go as myself. I can't think how Cousin Ophelia would justify her presence and going as Loony Lotte is out of the question, which is a shame because I rather like her. On second thought, she wouldn't have to explain her presence. She could just go into a rage."

"Yes, but I doubt Sterling would be willing to divulge any information to Loony Lotte. In any case, Tom and I will follow. We'll wait nearby." Evie surged to her feet and headed out of the library.

"What about us?" Henrietta asked. "Are we supposed to hold the fort?"

Sara plumped up her cushion. "Someone has to and thank goodness for that."

Toodles settled down by the fireplace. "What's this about Caro having an admirer?"

"Hurry," Tom mouthed as he caught up with Evie.

Evie rushed up the stairs to get her coat. In her room,

she found Millicent and Caro arguing over a pile of clothes.

"Excuse me." Evie dug around the pile and snatched a coat.

Caro took the coat from her and gave her another one.

"You might want these too, milady." Caro handed her a pair of gloves.

"And this scarf, milady," Millicent offered.

Not to be outdone, Caro produced a hat.

Millicent huffed. "Or perhaps her ladyship wants this hat."

"They're both quite suitable but I only have one head." Before they could present their arguments, Evie hurried away and left them to sort out their territorial disagreements by themselves.

She hoped the dowagers and Toodles didn't realize she had used following Lotte as an excuse to leave the house without anyone following her.

In her opinion, the police had the matter in hand and she and Tom no longer had a role to play in the investigation. However, if she told the others they would insist that she follow through and prod around for more information.

"Edgar, if we are not back for luncheon, please make an excuse for us. Feel free to say we telephoned and… decided to elope."

Edgar's lips parted and his eyes widened. "With all due respect, my lady. If I drop that particular bombshell, I might not be able to keep Lady Henrietta or Lady Sara or, indeed, Toodles, from setting off in pursuit of you."

"Fine, tell them we stopped at the pub for lunch."

Breathing a sigh of relief, Edgar nodded.

Tom must have seen the exchange from the motor car because when Evie settled in, he asked, "What did you say to poor Edgar?"

"It's how he reacted that should concern us. It seems we are not allowed to elope."

"Were we thinking of eloping?"

"It's an option. At least, it would have been." Evie slipped on her gloves. "I suppose we'll have to talk about it sometime."

"Before or after we find George Stevens' killer, the one we're not looking for because we're not really involved in the investigation?"

"On the other hand, it would be interesting to see what they did if we tried to elope."

He laughed.

Ahead, Lotte drove off in her motor car and they followed.

Evie sat back and thought about the storm several people had mentioned. The sky looked gray but not threatening. Maybe the storm they'd spoken of had been George Stevens' death.

Smiling to herself, she wondered if she should share her thoughts with Tom. That would add several more people to the list of suspects. Mr. Crooked Tie and his wife, Mrs. Mauve Dress. There had been another couple who'd mentioned the weather but she hadn't given them names.

Pulling her collar up, she also thought about George Stevens' wife. Had she known about his criminal activities or had she enjoyed blissful ignorance? Did she have any idea what had prompted her husband to attend a public event other than his desire to buy back a horse?

Evie even tried to grasp at straws. What if Mrs. Stevens had wanted her husband dead?

Heavens. There were so many possibilities, so many reasons for killing someone.

She tried to remember if Detective O'Neill had ever spoken about the perfect murder.

How would one succeed in killing someone and getting away with it?

No, Detective O'Neill always expected to find some sort of evidence. Something to lead him to the culprit. He didn't even like to contemplate the idea of someone getting away with murder.

They had done well to observe everyone at the ball. But what if they had missed someone obvious?

Tom slowed down. Looking up, Evie saw they had arrived at Hillsboro Lodge. Lotte had stopped ahead and Tom came to a stop beside her motor car.

"Is there anything in particular you'd like me to try to find out?" Lotte asked.

"The official cause of death." Evie really didn't want the horse to be responsible. "Did they find a vial? The poison must have been stored somewhere." Brightening, Evie said, "If they haven't found a vial on him or in his room, then that throws into the question the presence of the syringe."

Tom shifted. "Countess? You seem to like the idea of a conspiracy."

Evie shrugged. "Someone else put the syringe in the stall to throw suspicion off or point the finger at him and suggest George Stevens went to the stall to kill the horse. For all we know, someone lured him there and then planted evidence."

"Someone had the opportunity or created the opportunity," he said.

"Yes."

He looked at her for a moment. "It is possible the horse kicked him…"

"If that's the case, I'd prefer to think someone lured him inside the stall and startled Mighty Warrior. Oh, if you see the detective, you might want to mention rosebud green. With all the excitement last night, I think we forgot to tell him about it. Actually, I might have hesitated. Who knows what the detective would have made of my tale. And… we also want to know about the man who came with the platinum blonde woman." Evie nodded. "We'll wait for you."

They watched Lotte drive into the estate and then sat back to wait.

CHAPTER 20

The waiting game

Outside Hillsboro Lodge

om checked his watch.

Evie followed the gradual rise of his eyebrows and tried to read his expression. Either they'd only been waiting for a few minutes and that surprised him because it already felt like an eternity, or they had been sitting out in the motor car for longer than he'd thought.

"We've been out here for an hour," he said.

Alarmed by the news, Evie asked, "Do you think Lotte needs rescuing?"

"She can look after herself. At least, I hope she can. I'm actually surprised because we've been quiet for that long."

It took a moment for Evie to understand his meaning. She'd spent the time replaying everything that had happened over the last few days and she assumed he had been entertaining similar thoughts.

"Have we ever been silent for such a long stretch of time?" she asked.

"Not that I recall. Not even when we're in the library reading."

Her brows furrowed with concern. "Do I need to ask how you feel about that?"

"I'm just pleasantly surprised. You must admit, silence is rare at Halton House. There is always something happening."

"Yes, well… I might not have spoken but my mind simply wouldn't stop. How on earth did we find ourselves in this situation? Suddenly, I'm trying to think of ways to infiltrate the house and spy on people's conversations. Oh, and maybe rescue Lotte."

"No need. Here she comes."

Lotte stopped just outside the pillared gate, stuck her arm out and signaled to them.

"I think she wants us to follow."

They drove a short distance to the nearby village and stopped outside a pub. The Crooked Arrow boasted a menu of the best pies around.

"I hope Lotte has a lot to share with us over a lengthy luncheon. I'm not sure I'm ready to return to Halton House just yet," Evie revealed.

"Too much chaos?" Tom asked.

"We'll have to do something about restoring calm.

Everyone appears to be coming down with a bout of Henrietta's state of frenzy."

"A distraction could work," Tom suggested.

"Yes, perhaps we could set a date." Evie rolled her eyes. Heavens, that would involve so much planning. "We could pretend to elope and just disappear for a few days. I feel I need to catch my breath."

"That will not restore calm to the household," Tom warned.

"No, but it would work for me. Could I be a little selfish?"

"You wouldn't last the distance. You'd want to return in no time to set the record straight."

Lotte waited for them by the door. When they reached her, she pushed out a hard breath. "There is much to discuss."

Inside, they made their way to a table away from the people already enjoying an early lunch. The hum of conversation faded into the background as Lotte informed them of Marjorie Devon's efforts to clear her name.

"The detective is now focusing on her. According to Sterling Wright, Marjorie claims she went to the stables to check on the horse and that's when she ripped her dress."

"Has she been taken into custody?" Evie asked.

"No, she's still at Hillsboro Lodge but is not permitted to leave. The detective returned this morning and questioned her again."

Evie nodded. "That makes sense. It is difficult to keep lies straight and consistent."

"Where did you hear that?" Tom asked.

"I'm sure it's something Detective O'Neill said. If you

repeatedly question a suspect and they are guilty they are bound to slip up. The police use this tactic to pick up on inconsistencies. The fact she hasn't been taken into custody probably means the detective doesn't feel he has enough solid evidence to present a case. He needs to find a solid motive."

Lotte agreed. "Yet, I've met enough detectives who would have had a rope around her neck by now. As to the mysterious gentleman accompanied by the platinum blonde, he is visiting from America and looking to settle here. So, I doubt he is in any way involved in the murder."

"What about the others? Are they still at Hillsboro Lodge?"

Lotte nodded. "Everyone except Mrs. George Stevens. She returned to town early this morning. She has been taking prescribed narcotics to get her to sleep so the detective cleared her. In any case, according to Sterling Wright, the detective didn't have any doubts about Mrs. Stevens."

"And the others? How did they explain their absences from the ballroom?"

"They all said they were taking a break from the dancing."

"Did you speak with the detective?" Evie asked.

"No." Lotte looked around. "That's why we came here. Sterling Wright told me the detective is staying at the pub and has been having his meals here…" She checked her watch, "At about this time."

"And we are going to barge in on him," Tom said.

Lotte grinned. "Nonsense. We're going to invite him to join us. Here's something else. Everyone had their finger-prints taken."

"Really? What do they hope to match them with?"

"That's what I'm hoping the detective will tell us."

"And what about your investigation?" Evie asked.

"That, unfortunately, has now been closed. Sterling issued full payment for my services."

"Is that what took so long?"

"No. He spent most of the time telling me what happened after we left and also this morning."

In other words, he had talked a great deal without revealing anything they could use.

"He's worried about his reputation in the district. We already know he doesn't have his servants' loyalty."

Evie had never had that problem but she could imagine living in a house surrounded by people you couldn't trust would be quite uncomfortable and discouraging.

Hearing the entrance door opening, they all looked up. A group of locals walked in and settled at a table.

Lotte resumed telling her tale. "After Sterling concluded our business, I assumed he would show me the door but, instead, he offered me coffee. I thought the others would join us but they were out riding."

"Without a care in the world," Evie mused.

"Yes. If any of them are guilty, they deserve a prize for their brazen audacity."

Tom looked at Evie. "If your theory about a conspiracy is correct, they might want to stay close to the scene of the crime to make sure Marjorie sticks to her story."

Not much of a theory, Evie thought, since she hadn't been able to come up with a motive.

Most of the guests they had identified as possible

suspects had shared interests in horse racing. But that didn't include Marjorie Devon.

"Here he is." Lotte jumped to her feet and waved. "Detective, do come and join us."

Evie turned in time to see the detective hesitate. He glanced around the pub and then appeared resigned to his fate. Nodding, he removed his hat and walked toward them, his steps showing a hint of reluctance.

He greeted them and sat next to Lotte. "What brings you out this way?"

Lotte explained about her business with Sterling Wright and also revealed the fact they knew about the fabric found in the stables.

He reorganized his cutlery and Evie imagined him trying to avoid the subject. Had he had a change of heart about sharing information with them?

"Did you ask Marjorie about *rosebud green* or did we forget to tell you about it?" Lotte didn't wait for his reply and went on to explain how Evie had come across the note. "You must admit Lady Woodridge did well to discover it. We have pinpointed the location."

He blinked several times before saying, "It's worth looking into."

"But?" Lotte pushed.

He sighed. "At the moment, our investigation is focused on interviewing some of the guests. We are also looking into their background."

Evie leaned forward. "You are trying to find a connection between them and George Stevens?"

"Yes. We know they are all linked to the world of horseracing but that doesn't necessarily mean they have been in any way connected with George Stevens. What we need to find now is a motive. We don't have a weapon. Finding a motive is essential in such a case."

Because, otherwise, this would be a random killing, Evie thought.

"Did you find out what happened to the stable hands?"

He shook his head. "They have a small kitchen above the stables. The milk has been sent for analysis."

"If you had to guess?" Lotte asked.

"I'd say someone put a sleeping powder in the milk. Someone who learned their routine. One of the stable lads said he talked to a man but he couldn't describe him. He said he looked like a regular bloke. The lad thought he'd come with the guests so he didn't think anything of it."

"What sort of questions did he ask?"

"He showed an interest in how they were treated. If they had a good life there. The boy said he was well fed and felt lucky to have a warm bed to sleep in every night."

"Did he ask about their routine?"

"The boy said something about early to bed, early to rise."

Evie told him about the man they had seen talking with Helena Lloyd during the foxhunt. "We didn't get a good look at him but I don't think he was a guest."

The detective shrugged. "It could be someone working behind the scenes."

Did that make Helena Lloyd a strong suspect?

The detective smiled. "Or, Mrs. Lloyd might have been having a tryst." He studied Evie for a moment. "However, the encounter has been taken into account."

"I heard some of the guests had their fingerprints taken," Lotte said.

The detective closed his eye briefly. Evie guessed he was trying to call for calm.

"You heard correctly."

"Does that mean you found a fingerprint?"

"Indeed."

Evie grinned. "And you are going to make us work really hard to get the information out of you."

"I sent the syringe to Scotland Yard. They contacted me this morning to say they had found a partial print which could be used to identify the culprit. Of course, they needed samples of fingerprints. We took care of that and sent the information on."

"And now you have to wait to hear from Scotland Yard," Evie mused. "Thank heavens none of us handled the syringe."

The more she thought about it, the more Evie believed someone had gone to a great deal of trouble to plan the murder.

The detective appeared to relax.

Lotte knew she had the tiger by the tail and clearly refused to let go. "What about the cause of death?"

He brushed a hand across his brow. Evie found his patience admirable. She knew he was under no obligation to share what he knew with them.

"We initially suspected he suffered a severe kick to the head. However, the examiner has now found evidence of another blow made with a small instrument."

"Something like a hammer?" Lotte asked.

"Possibly."

Evie sat back and pushed out a sigh of relief. That put the horse in the clear. "Rosebud Green," Evie said and thought she saw the detective's eye twitch.

"All in due course, my lady. We do have a process of elimination. Unfortunately, we also have a scarcity of personnel. It is my job to delegate responsibilities and people can't be everywhere at once." He sighed again. "You don't look convinced. Rest assured, we will investigate Rosebud Green."

"Just not today." Evie suddenly understood Henrietta's impatience.

They placed their orders. Despite not being hungry, Evie went ahead and ordered a game pie.

"What about Archie Arthurs? Has he turned up?" Evie asked.

The detective shook his head. "His luggage is still at Hillsboro Lodge. No one has seen him since the morning of the ball. Sterling Wright assures me there is nothing unusual in his disappearance as he has a habit of wandering off. Mr. Wright is convinced he will turn up eventually. We hope he does. There is something suspicious about his behavior and we would like to speak with him."

Evie drummed her fingers on the table and tried to remember what else they had discussed.

The vial.

When she asked him about it, the detective sat back and studied her for a moment. "We didn't find one."

That took everyone by surprise.

"That does open up a new avenue. The poison must have been stored somewhere."

When he made a note of it, Evie knew the idea hadn't occurred to him.

Putting his notebook aside, he asked, "How is Lady Carolina?"

Evie couldn't decide if he wanted to change the subject, if he'd asked out of politeness or if he had a special interest in Caro's wellbeing. "She is doing her best to remember something that might help you in your investigation."

When their meals were served, they focused on summarizing everything they had observed, giving the detective no chance to enjoy a quiet meal.

The moment they finished their meal, the detective shot to his feet and excused himself.

As they parted ways, Tom murmured, "The detective is clutching his stomach. I think we might have given him a bout of indigestion."

"What now?" Lotte asked.

"We could enjoy a drive in the country," Evie suggested.

Both Tom and Lotte looked up at the gray sky.

"Do you have any particular destination in mind?" Tom asked even though he already knew the answer.

"Yes, the village of Rosebud Green."

CHAPTER 21

A drive in the country

Rosebud Green

Smaller than the village of Halton, Rosebud Green had a row of buildings with various businesses and dwellings above. They had spotted a couple of large manor houses along the way and could see one at the end of the main street. A church spire rose above another row of buildings. And, peeking from around the corner, they saw the edge of what looked like a village green, which no doubt led to the church.

"This does not look like a hub of criminal activity," Evie observed.

Tom laughed. "Is that what you hoped to find?"

"I'm now worried. The detective has few resources at his disposal. How... When is he going to find the time to scour through the village and surrounding countryside?"

Tom looked up at the sky. "Is that what we're going to do? We might need to revise our plans."

"We should be finished before those dark clouds decide what they want to do."

Stopping outside a tearoom, they waited for Lotte to join them. When she did, she suggested walking around.

After surveying the length and breath of the village, they returned to the tearoom.

"The church is pretty," Evie said. "And I'm sure some of these buildings date back to Tudor times. It would all be interesting enough if we were here to take in the sights. Shall we go in for refreshments? We could ask if there have been any strangers visiting lately."

"I'm willing to bet we'll be the only ones," Lotte said. "You would need to be quite adventurous to find this village."

Inside, they went to stand by the fireplace to warm up. There were three women enjoying their afternoon tea with scones. A young woman hurried in from the back of the establishment carrying a tray with more scones. She smiled and invited them to sit wherever they liked.

Since a table by the window offered them a view of the road, they sat there.

"I suppose I can understand why the detective didn't sound in a hurry to come here."

Lotte nodded. "He would need a strong lead to justify the trip. He has already questioned the guests, including Marjorie who left a piece of her dress in the stables. The detective still hasn't made an arrest. Yet, he is determined to continue questioning the guests and waiting for test results to return. He probably has to justify his every move to a higher authority. Whereas we are free to roam about and follow our curiosity."

Evie twirled her thumbs. She looked at Lotte. "I keep going back to the conversations you overhead. I'm trying to justify my theory about a conspiracy."

Lotte nodded. "*You are going to ruin us*. From memory, that's what I overheard Helena Lloyd say."

Evie nodded. "Now I'm thinking about Twiggy Lloyd's red face when he returned to the great hall. That's when I noticed Sterling Wright had also been missing. When he walked in, his gaze went straight to Twiggy."

"Do you think Sterling is involved?" Tom asked.

"Perhaps not in a crime. My imagination tells me he stumbled on a plot and tried to call those involved to order. He seemed determined to ignore George Stevens' efforts to buy back the horse. Maybe he is the type to want to step back and let things play out without taking any action. And, maybe, when he discovered the others had taken action…"

"He intervened," Tom said.

"Yes… Maybe." Evie waved her hands. "Imagination serves a purpose up to a point. The detective said he's looking into the guests' backgrounds. He wants something solid to pursue."

As soon as the young woman came to take their orders, Lotte asked, "Do you get many visitors to the area?"

"Not at this time of the year. In the springtime, we hold several fairs but that only attracts local farmers." She tilted her head. "Actually, it's funny you should ask. Someone asked the same question earlier today."

"Really? A man or a woman?"

She nodded. "A woman. There were two of them. A lady and her maid. Now that I think about it, they were joined by the chauffeur, which I found unusual. I've never seen the local gentry coming in with their servants."

"What did you tell them?"

She smiled and seemed quite happy to chat with them. "The same thing I told you. Except… they pressed me for more information."

"And did you have anything further to add?"

"No, not really. But they were keen to get some information out of me. That's when they started rattling off names to see if I recognized any of them."

They all looked intrigued.

"Can you remember any of the names they mentioned?" Tom asked.

"Let me think… There was one name I found amusing. Twiggy something or other."

"Twiggy Lloyd?"

Her eyes widened with surprise. "Yes, that's it."

"What about the other names?"

"Let me think… Oh, yes. They mentioned Archie Arthurs."

When the young woman didn't explain further, Tom pressed her, "And the name sounded familiar?"

"Not exactly. I mean… I heard someone being called Mr. Arthurs. That seemed to interest the lady. Mr. Arthurs came in for a cup of tea and another man walked in soon afterward and called out his name." The young woman cleared her throat and deepening her voice, said, "Mr. Arthurs. We're ready."

We're ready?

Ready for what?

"This happened today?" Lotte asked.

"No, that was yesterday."

"In the morning or the afternoon? Can you recall?"

"Close to midmorning."

Archie Arthurs hadn't been at the ball. Had he been absent for longer than an afternoon and evening? Had he left Hillsboro Lodge in the morning? The detective had told them he'd left his luggage behind which suggested he would eventually return.

Lotte persevered. "Do you remember hearing them talk about anything?"

"No. However, Roy Chandler might be able to help you. He came in later in the afternoon and mentioned the men. Roy works in the store next door. He said they had asked about Linton House. That's when we concluded they were here to buy a horse."

Lotte frowned. "Why did you think that?"

"Because Linton House has fine stables and the owner is always selling horses."

"Where is this place?"

"Not far from the village."

Evie leaned forward. "What about the lady and her maid. Did you happen to hear their names?"

The young woman giggled. "Yes, the maid had a sarcastic tone when she called the other woman Lady. Let me think… Oh, yes. Lady Carolina."

Caro?

"Are you sure?"

The young woman nodded. "Well, perhaps not sarcastic. More like… mocking. Yes, I had the impression the maid was making fun of her."

That sounded like Millicent.

What on earth had come over Caro and Millicent? Why had they come here?

Shaking her head, Evie asked, "What happened after you told them about Mr. Arthurs?"

"They left. In fact, they hurried out."

Had they returned to Halton House? "How long ago was that?"

The young woman looked over her shoulder at the clock hanging behind the counter. "About an hour ago."

"And where exactly is Linton House?" Lotte asked.

"You follow the road and at the first turn you follow that road and you'll soon see an entrance on the right with red brick pillars. One has an urn and the other has a statue of a horse."

Tom dug inside his pocket and drew out some money. "For your troubles."

They all surged to their feet and hurried out of the establishment.

Evie couldn't stop shaking her head. "What on earth is Caro thinking?"

"We'll soon find out," Lotte said in a determined tone.

Evie worried they might be wasting time. "What if Caro came to her senses and returned to Halton House?"

Lotte snorted. "Really? I'm more inclined to think your maid has been struck by a sudden need for adventure."

As they sped off, Evie growled under her breath. "I refuse to think something has happened to Caro and

Millicent. Honestly, when I get my hands on them, I'll… Well, I'll be very cross."

"Relax, Countess. They have Edmonds with them."

"I need to get my house under control," Evie fumed. "I've obviously been too lenient."

"Spare the rod, spoil the maid?"

Evie shook her head. "This is not like Caro. She is constantly telling me to take care. Honestly, when I told her about my intentions to become a fully-fledged lady detective, I thought she would have an attack of nerves. What is she trying to prove? Oh, heavens. Do you think she is trying to prove something?"

Tom laughed. "My apologies, Countess. I can't stop thinking about Millicent's mocking tone. I think she must have been unhappy about playing the role of lady's maid."

Evie groaned and then laughed. "Yes, I can easily picture Millicent arguing and wanting a turn at being a lady."

Just as they cleared the village, they spotted a vehicle traveling at great speed and heading their way.

"I don't want to alarm you," Tom said, "but I think that is a police vehicle." He slowed down and the other motor car appeared to do so as well.

When it reached them, the driver looked out the window.

"It's the detective," Evie exclaimed.

Everyone stopped in the middle of the road and Tom and the detective jumped out.

Evie couldn't hear the conversation. Had the detective changed his mind about spreading his investigation to Rosebud Green? Or had something unexpected happened? When she noticed he had come alone, Evie scooped in a calming breath. Perhaps he was on some sort of unofficial trip.

Evie turned and saw Lotte patiently waiting to see what would happen next. Glancing over at Tom, Evie saw him give a stiff nod. He hurried back and before he could settle in, Evie demanded, "What's happened?"

Tom waited for the detective to turn his vehicle around and then followed him. "After our lunch with the detective, he returned to the police station to see if there were any messages from Scotland Yard. Instead, he was given a message from Halton House."

Evie gasped. "Good heavens."

"Not knowing how to contact the detective, Edgar telephoned the local constabulary and they relayed the message. Your butler tried to stop Caro and when she insisted on driving out to Rosebud Green, he worried she might be getting in over her head." Tom turned slightly and smiled at Evie. "You'll be pleased to know the detective wasted no time in setting out here when he heard Caro might be headed for danger. He is beside himself with worry."

"A knight in shining armor?"

"Indeed. I should add, he is not at all pleased with you."

"*Me?* What did I do?"

"You let your servants run amok. He thinks you are too soft on them. Don't be offended, but I believe I heard him murmur something about problems arising when titles fall in the hands of the wrong people."

"He thinks I'm not good enough to have a title? I suppose I must make concessions for him because he is overly concerned about Caro's wellbeing."

"And that is your failing. You shouldn't concern yourself so much with other people's feelings. Remember, you are the Countess of Woodridge. Wield that rod with no mercy, Countess."

"I'm glad you find this amusing." After a moment, she huffed out, "Thank you. For a moment, you managed to take my mind off this worrying business. I pray we don't find Caro here. It's been over an hour and she must surely be on her way back to Halton House. Yes, that's what she must have done. I'm sure she did. For her sake, I hope she did."

Shuddering, Evie brushed her gloved hands across her face. So many things could have happened in an hour. She would throttle her maid. At least, she ought to…

Pushing out a breath, she opened her eyes and stared straight ahead. "Why is he slowing down? Is he slowing down? He is slowing down. Why?"

They all came to a stop. Evie looked over her shoulder and saw Lotte bringing her motor car to a stop too.

The detective emerged from his motor and trotted over to them. Leaning in, he said, "We'll need more people. We don't know what's up ahead."

Evie felt somewhat comforted by his inclusion. She would hate to feel the need to kick up a fuss if he told her to stay out of the way. Of course, she wouldn't get in the way, nor would she remain behind. Especially not now. Did he think Caro had gone to Linton House? Evie insisted on believing her maid had more sense than that.

Lotte joined them. "What's happened? Why did you stop?"

Tom looked up at her. "Someone needs to alert the local constabulary."

"I guess that someone should be me," Lotte volunteered. She looked back toward the village. "Are they likely to have a police presence in that small village?"

The detective's voice filled with urgency. "Probably not, but that will be a good place to start. I'm sure someone will point you in the right direction."

Giving a firm nod, Lotte rushed back to her motor car and took off toward the village.

Back on the road, they reached the first turn. Evie saw a house in the distance but then she lost sight of it. Her fingers curled into the palms of her hands. What would they find? Anything could happen in an hour. If Caro had set out this way, Evie prayed she had been sensible enough to go no further than the road. Her maid always warned her against taking unnecessary risks. Why had she ventured out? Had Henrietta urged her on?

"I have a riding crop I can use," she murmured. "Yes, I'm going to start walking around with a riding crop. Henrietta has her umbrella, I'll have my riding crop. They will come to fear me. I will be known as the wrathful Countess. She who must be feared."

Tom pointed ahead. "We're here."

The detective brought his motor car to a stop, well away from the gate. He rushed toward them. "I will approach on foot and see if I can spot their vehicle. Do you have any idea what they are driving?"

Tom nodded. "The Duesenberg. You won't have any trouble identifying it."

The detective nodded. "Meanwhile, you two stay here."

"But what will you do if you see the motor car?" Evie asked. "From what we understand, Caro is in character and playing the role of Lady Carolina. I imagine she has contrived some sort of story to get inside and look around."

"Let's hope that's the case." The detective rushed back to his car, retrieved something and then made his way along the entrance.

"Heavens, I think he is now armed." Evie closed her eyes and, after a moment, she asked, "What's happening?"

"He just cleared the gate. Give him time."

Nodding, she forced herself to focus on Archie Arthurs. Had he left Hillsboro Lodge on the day of the ball? To do what? Why had he come here? This couldn't be a coincidence.

The young woman at the tearooms had said the owner sold horses. Could his trip have been about the purchase of a horse? If not for the fact someone had been killed, Evie would be inclined to think they were barking up the wrong tree.

"This can't be a coincidence," Evie murmured. "And, yes, this is what Detective Inspector O'Neill would say."

They kept their eyes peeled on the pillared entrance.

"How long are we going to wait before we decide we have to do something?" Evie considered pulling her glove off so she could nibble on the tip of her thumb but if she wanted to wield a riding crop and restore order to her household, she would have to curtail the habit. That made her laugh.

"Did I miss something?" Tom asked.

"I'm trying to distract myself."

"It's obviously working."

Not for long, she thought. "If Archie Arthurs came here yesterday, he is now long gone." Evie hoped that was the case. "Now I'm thinking this will cast a bad light on

Caro. The detective came to her rescue. With Archie Arthurs not here, the detective will have wasted his time." She stared ahead and prayed Archie Arthurs had returned to Hillsboro Lodge only to realize her prayer wouldn't be answered. The man had come here yesterday and, this morning, he had yet to make an appearance at Hillsboro Lodge.

Tom smiled at her. "But he will have won Caro's heart."

It took a moment for Evie to understand what he meant. She managed to smile but it quickly faded. Telling him about her thoughts, Evie shivered.

"That's the problem with playing around with ideas," Tom said. "Your hopes and expectations intrude and thwart reality."

"We should go in and see what's happened. He's been gone long enough."

"What happened to not interfering in police business?"

"I lied. Besides, this involves Caro."

"We should at least wait for Lotte to return."

Evie's finger shot out. "He's coming."

Instead of heading for them, the detective went straight to his motor car and signaled for them to follow him.

Evie gasped. "My heart is thumping all the way to my throat."

"Yes, mine is beating the same tune."

The driveway cut through the parkland and led them straight to the manor house. The Georgian building looked well maintained. Evie knew only too well what it cost to keep these houses from crumbling. She'd heard of some owners being forced to close rooms because they couldn't afford to repair the roof. If not seen to, from one year to the next, the damage incurred after the rain and snow would be enough to exacerbate the situation, increasing the cost of repairs. Many houses had met their end that way. This one had clearly evaded that fate.

"There's Edmonds." He stood by the motor car. Evie watched for any signs of uneasiness and saw none.

"I have no idea what to expect."

"Nor do I." Tom stopped the motor alongside the Duesenberg.

Ambling toward them, Edmonds gave Evie an uneasy smile. "My lady. They are unharmed."

"Edmonds, what on earth has been going on here? From what we understand, you came here an hour ago."

"Yes, however, we spent some time at the gates debating what to do. In the end, Caro suggested we should pretend the motor broke down. I had to push it all the way up the driveway. The owner offered Caro and Millicent refreshments while I fixed the motor."

"I take it you managed to fix it," Evie said.

Edmonds looked confused. "There was nothing wrong with it, my lady."

Turning to Tom, Evie said, "So, how are we going to explain our arrival with the detective, no less."

"Begging your pardon, my lady. Caro has already thought of that. She is pretending to be a runaway bride being forced into marriage against her will and has been on the road traveling to a distant relative's house to seek refuge and support."

Evie and Tom stared at him, their mouths gaping open.

"Since we didn't know what we would find here, she even thought to bring along some luggage."

Evie could only imagine the sudden upheaval at Halton House with everyone rushing around trying to prepare things for Caro's departure.

Tom smiled. "And, here we are, chasing after her and without a spare change of clothes. What are we to do if we don't succeed in convincing her to return with us? We have even taken the precaution of bringing the police. But that might not be enough."

"I'm glad you find this amusing." Evie stared at the house and tried to imagine the scene inside. "That won't do at all. The detective will have to play another role."

Shaking his head, Tom said, "I'll leave it up to you to tell him."

CHAPTER 22

The end of the road

On the doorstep of Linton House

"Caro could be in danger," Evie urged. "Detective, you have to pretend to be a concerned relative."

Even as they stood at the door ready to make their presence known, the detective didn't look convinced.

"My lady, do I need to remind you this is a murder investigation? Perhaps I should pretend to be here to arrest Lady Carolina."

Evie studied him. He'd sounded serious so she assumed he had to be serious.

The detective looked up and pushed out a breath.

"Actually, you might be right. Yes, it will be best to avoid the truth. For all we know, the owner of the house might be involved in George Stevens' death."

"Marvelous," Evie exclaimed.

The detective adjusted his tie. "So, Caro is running away from a forced marriage and I'm playing the role of…"

"Knight in shining armor. You don't need to worry about Caro. She'll pick up on our ruse and play along. By the way… What is your first name?"

"Henry." The detective adjusted his tie again. "I'm just not sure what I'm supposed to do."

"Jump to her defense, of course. Promise her the moon. Trust me, she'll take it."

"She'll think I'm mad."

Evie gave him an impish smile. The fact he cared what Caro thought of him said a great deal. Probably more than he wished others to know.

Tom cleared his throat. "Just remember, we are here to extricate Caro and Millicent from whatever trouble they have landed themselves in. I'm sure Caro has been asking questions that might have triggered some suspicions."

An elderly butler answered the door, his bushy eyebrows rising a notch as he took in the trio standing at the door. After a moment of silent deliberation, he showed them through to a drawing room.

Millicent sat by the door, her lips pursed, her eyebrows drawn down, while Caro sat near the fireplace enjoying a cup of tea.

A man with a wild mop of graying hair sat opposite her.

When the butler announced their presence, Caro's cup

rattled. She turned and nearly sent the cup crashing down.

"My heavens, what are you doing here?" Caro asked, her tone clipped.

"Dear Cousin Carolina," Evie walked up to her. "Thank goodness we have found you. We have come here to talk sense into you."

The man rose to his feet and introduced himself as Mr. Buckton.

Evie apologized for the intrusion. Tom and the detective stepped forward and she introduced them. "This is Mr. Tom Winchester and this is Mr. Henry Evans."

Caro had only half turned. When she heard the detective's name, her cup rattled again. Evie thought she saw her mouthing the detective's name.

"We are glad you haven't come to any harm," Evie continued. "Everyone has been so worried." As she spoke, Evie studied the man. He didn't strike her as someone who would be involved in the criminal world. Then again, George Stevens hadn't looked like a criminal either.

"Mr. Buckton has been kind enough to entertain me while Edmonds fixes the motor car. He was about to give me a tour of his house."

"I'm sure you have imposed on his kindness long enough, Cousin Carolina. We really should be on our way."

"But I'm not sure I'm ready to return." Caro's eyebrows hitched up slightly.

Evie sent the man an apologetic smile. "I'm sure Mr. Buckton does not wish to hear about our family squabbles."

"Oh, but it's too late. He knows all about our dirty laundry. Besides, he has promised to show me his stables."

Would Caro insist on seeing the stables if she didn't think it would be safe to do so? She had always been quick to object to anything that might put her in danger.

"I would be more than happy to show you the stables, my lady. Your cousin has been telling me you have developed an interest in racing horses."

Looking at Caro, Evie beseeched her, "If we do this, will you promise you will return with us?"

Caro glanced at the detective. "Perhaps."

"Follow me," Mr. Buckton invited.

They filed out of the drawing room and followed Mr. Buckton out of the house.

Tom and the detective walked behind her. Glancing over her shoulder, Evie saw them surveying the area.

Mr. Buckton held the stables' door open for them. As they moved through the threshold, Evie tensed. Suddenly, she became aware of the possibility of walking straight into danger.

"You have quite a stable here, Mr. Buckton," Evie said.

"We had them restored a couple of years ago so most of it looks quite new."

She had been referring to the horses. There had to be over twenty, perhaps more. "They're all racing horses?"

He nodded.

She walked the length of the stables reading the name plates on the stall doors. Finally, she came to one without a name. She turned to look at him.

"Unfortunately, that's not one of mine." He explained how he had been approached the day before to stable a horse temporarily. "They suffered a similar fate to your cousin and broke down not far from here."

The others walked up for a closer look.

"He's a lovely chestnut…" Mr. Buckton broke off and turned toward the stable doors. The sound of running footsteps headed toward them had everyone else turning.

A moment later, several constables burst in waving their truncheons and blowing their whistles.

"What in heaven's name is this about?" Mr. Buckton demanded.

"I believe, sir, you are in possession of stolen property," Evie said.

~

Moments later...

Leaving the local constabulary to deal with the situation, they returned to their vehicles and headed back to Hillsboro Lodge.

"It seems the answer lay with Rosebud Green all along," Evie said. The detective didn't know it yet, but they were following him back to Hillsboro Lodge.

"You should get a special commendation for this," Tom said.

"No one has been arrested yet."

"But you recovered a horse no one knew had been missing."

"That is strange. How did Sterling Wright not realize he had a different horse in his stable?"

"Didn't you say he had been vague when he'd talked about Mighty Warrior?"

"Yes and, even after only meeting him once before, I had the impression he didn't really know much about horses. Of course, I might have been wrong since he said he has a hand in training them. Perhaps he simply doesn't possess an eye for detail. Or, maybe, he hasn't been to the stables since his new horse arrived."

"That's a possibility."

During the half hour drive back, Evie tried to piece together a theory that would make sense.

Archie Arthurs had stolen the horse from right under Sterling's nose. The theft had to be connected to George Stevens' death.

Evie shook her head.

"What's wrong?" Tom asked.

"If you repeat a word enough times, it soon loses all meaning. I'm experiencing the same dilemma with the information we've been collecting."

The four motor cars drove through the gates leading to Hillsboro Lodge. Evie expected the detective to stop and tell them to turn back. When he didn't, they continued to follow him.

As they came to a stop, they saw a rider galloping toward the house.

Sterling Wright.

The detective stood by his motor car and waited for him. When Sterling dismounted, the detective approached him.

Evie nudged Tom and they walked toward them. If the detective saw them coming, he didn't stop them.

They heard him say, "I would like to ask you a few questions about Mr. Arthurs."

Sterling handed the reins to a stable boy. "Archie? What about him?"

"When was the last time you saw him?"

"About an hour ago. He's inside. In fact, your detectives are talking with him right now."

The detective rushed inside. Sterling Wright looked at Evie and Tom. "Would someone mind telling me what's going on?"

"Have you seen Mighty Warrior since he arrived?" Evie asked.

He nodded. "Briefly."

"Did you see him up close?"

"No, it's been rather busy what with the hunt and the ball and I've spent most of today trying to clear my head."

"I think you might want to go to the stables," Evie suggested.

The others caught up with them and followed them to the stables.

"What's this about?" Sterling asked. He pushed the stable doors open and walked in.

The impostor Mighty Warrior snorted.

Even with the stable doors open, the light was quite poor. "I think you might want to take a close look at him."

He did, however, after a moment, instead of noticing the different coloring, as Evie had hoped he would, he noticed the horse's frame. In his opinion, it was wider than he remembered.

"What's going on here?"

"We believe your horse has been swapped." Evie swung away and walked outside.

Following her, Tom murmured, "George Stevens would have been able to identify him."

"Yes, the thought only now took shape in my mind. He might have been killed for that very reason. Although, that still doesn't tell us who killed him."

Archie Arthurs had organized to swap the horse but someone had assisted him. How had he known where to intercept it and when?

Evie felt they had been witnesses to a crime but she had no idea how to interpret what they had seen.

Turning, she saw Sterling had joined them outside. He looked dumbfounded.

Plucking out one of the many snippets of information she had floating around her mind, she asked, "Does the room opposite the library face the stables?"

Sterling hesitated. He looked up at the house, almost as if he needed to think about it. "Yes, I believe it does."

Turning to Tom, she said, "Caro said she thought there had been a third person in the room opposite the library. I think Archie Arthurs was here all along keeping an eye on the stables. He just didn't make an appearance at the ball. We know he went to Rosebud Green, but then he might have returned during the evening."

"Rosebud Green?" Sterling asked. "Didn't you ask me about that the other day at dinner?"

"Yes, and you said it sounded familiar."

Sterling looked up at the house again. "Yes, at the time, I didn't remember where I'd heard it mentioned but it's come back to me now. The drivers transporting Mighty Warrior had been in touch with me. They said he had been skittish and might injure himself so they were going to stop at Rosebud Green overnight or however long it took to calm him down."

"Can you remember when you had that conversation?" Evie asked.

He raked his fingers through his hair. "The day of the dinner."

"The day I attended the foxhunt."

Sterling nodded.

It had also been the day Marjorie Devon had gone to Mrs. Green's establishment. Evie had only just discovered Lotte had decided to dress as her cousin. Shortly after, Caro had received a telephone call from Mrs. Green alerting her of Marjorie's imminent arrival at her establishment. Despite not finding her there, Evie had found the piece of paper…

Marjorie must have heard Sterling mentioning the place or perhaps she had overheard the telephone conversation.

Had she then told Archie Arthurs and had he used the information to set up his heist?

Why would she share that information? What role did Marjorie play?

The detective had said he had to look into everyone's background. With this sort of information, she thought he might be able to focus his search. Who would stand to gain the most by taking possession of a valuable horse?

Some or all of the guests they had suspected might have had a stake in Mighty Warrior's kidnapping.

The snippets of conversations Lotte had overheard during her overnight stay at Hillsboro Lodge came back to her.

She turned to Sterling. "If Twiggy Lloyd owned a share of Mighty Warrior, would he have the right to sell the horse?"

"It would be ungentlemanly of him to do so without letting me know. He'd need a majority share…" Sterling broke off and looked toward the house again.

"Have others approached you about buying a share?" She remembered him mentioning Matthew Prentiss' interest.

Sterling still held his riding crop in his hand. Evie saw his fingers tightening around it. If anything, his reaction suggested he had not been involved in something underhanded.

He gave a stiff nod.

After taking a close look at the horse, Sterling had realized he had a different horse. Surely the perpetrators could not have expected to get away with switching horses.

When they had learned of George Stevens' visit, they must have panicked. Had he been killed because they thought he alone could identify Mighty Warrior?

Lowering her voice, she said, "Maybe they thought they would get away with stealing Mighty Warrior by killing this horse." But they hadn't succeeded. Had someone caught them in the act?

"Do you really think Sterling would not have realized it wasn't Mighty Warrior?" Tom asked.

"Who knows what goes through a criminal's mind. Those are the sort of mistakes that prevent people from getting away with murder. Which is precisely what has happened here."

Earlier, she had told Tom they should stop thinking about the letters because they were distracting. However, she couldn't help bringing them up again.

Looking at Sterling, she said, "Marjorie received more than one threatening letter but you only produced one for Lotte's perusal."

He looked at her, his eyebrows drawn down.

"You didn't ask Lotte to find out who sent them because… I think you already know who sent them and if Lotte had seen those other letters, she would have discovered the person's identity." And, Evie thought, for some reason, Sterling hadn't wanted that to happen.

Evie turned and glanced at Lotte who appeared to be in deep thought. Millicent and Caro stood behind her, their lips slightly parted as if they couldn't quite believe what they were witnessing.

They heard a commotion coming from the front of the house. They all made their way there and saw two detectives leading Archie Arthurs away.

His protests were loud and clear. They wouldn't be able to prove anything. They didn't have any witnesses.

"If the detective's lucky, Archie Arthurs' fingerprints will match the one on the syringe," Tom said.

Evie watched the detective as he walked toward them. She would leave it up to Sterling Wright to reveal the information he held about the letters.

"Archie Arthurs sounds sure of himself," Evie said.

The detective shook his head. "No doubt he thinks others will cover for him."

"I think you have your man, detective. And I'm sure the others involved will want to co-operate with you."

Evie sensed her shoulders easing down. She turned to look at Caro and Millicent. They both took a step back.

Smiling, Tom asked, "What now, Countess?"

"Now? Now we'll have to explain everything to the others. I haven't decided if I will do that before or after I give them a piece of my mind. Then again, I could delay everything until we hear back from the detective. I'm sure the fingerprints will match."

"And the letters?"

Turning, she saw Sterling Wright talking with the detective. He'd said he needed to look into everyone's background where he felt he would find something to indicate a strong motive. Evie felt sure he would find something in those letters.

"But why had Marjorie pretended she didn't know who'd written them? Had she been in denial?"

"Countess? Are you thinking out loud again?"

"Yes. What would push Marjorie Devon into risking everything? Despite losing her fiancé in the war, she had managed to find another one, and a wealthy one at that. Why did she do this to him?"

Lotte crossed her arms and hummed. "Marjorie Devon's father is a banker."

"Yes, I remember you telling us. Do you suspect him of pressuring his daughter into playing a role in switching the horses? Why would he do that?"

"Strange," Lotte mused, "a moment ago, I would have sworn you thought her father had something to do with it all. Even without mentioning him."

Evie pushed out a breath. "I'm exhausted. I think it's time to head back to Halton House."

Hearing this, Millicent and Caro scurried away.

"I think they're going to be out of sight for a while," Tom said.

Evie smiled. "Good. I need them to fear me. But I won't be too hard on them." She glanced over her shoulder at the detective. "After all, I might need to use Caro as bait."

CHAPTER 23

Halton House
Two days later...

$\mathcal{E}$vie walked into the drawing room. Stopping in the middle of the room, she tapped her riding crop against her leg. "Edgar?"

Her butler appeared at the door. "My lady?"

"Some tea, please."

Tom entered, made his way to a chair and sat down with a huff. "That was an invigorating stroll around the park. I wonder if there is a single member of your household who didn't stand by a window to watch us. Can you imagine them trying to read your lips?"

Evie smiled. "You put on quite a performance, flailing your arms about and stomping off."

"I thought we should give them something to talk

about. Edgar has probably rushed off to tell them all is well. How long are we going to keep this up?"

Hearing a rush of footsteps coming toward them, they both looked up. Henrietta burst in. "Here you are at last. This must stop. I don't understand why we are being punished."

"No one is punishing you, Henrietta." Evie tapped her riding crop against her thigh.

"We simply cannot go on like this," Henrietta complained. "You cannot keep us in the dark."

"Yes, I can." Evie nodded and tapped her riding crop for added effect. "You sent Caro and Millicent off on what could have turned into a dangerous adventure."

"But nothing happened to them. It's been two days and you still refuse to tell us what happened."

Evie tilted her head. "What about your spies?"

"They are being fed lies. Someone has made sure of that."

Evie took a chair opposite Tom who hadn't stopped smiling. "Do sit down, Henrietta. We're about to have some tea. Where are the others?"

Henrietta lifted her chin. "They were here a moment ago, but when they heard you heading this way, they fled to the library. You have us all on tenterhooks."

Evie grinned. "I can't imagine Toodles being on tenterhooks. You should ask them to join us."

Edgar came into the drawing followed by a footman carrying the tea tray. "My lady. Detective Inspector Evans has arrived."

"Thank you, Edgar. Show him through." Finally, she thought. The detective had telephone earlier to ask if he could speak with Lady Carolina and Evie had taken the opportunity to bargain with him. The fact he had made the request could only mean he had finally closed the case.

Henrietta lowered herself into the nearest chair. "Edgar, please let Lady Sara, Toodles and Lotte know we are about to have tea in the drawing room."

Evie hid her smile. She knew nothing would budge Henrietta from her front row seat.

The detective appeared at the door and glanced around the room.

"Come in, detective," Evie invited. "How wonderful to see you again." She noticed the detective had dressed in country tweeds instead of a gray suit. "What news do you bring?"

Tom disguised his laughter with a cough.

"Have some tea, Tom. That couch sounds serious."

Evie stood up and poured herself a cup of tea. As she turned, she noticed the detective looking toward the door. He could not have looked more disappointed when Toodles, Lotte and Sara entered the library.

Pretending not to have noticed Evie, Toodles asked, "Is it safe?"

Evie gave her a bright smile. "Grans, just in time for tea. Mind where you seat, please. I left my riding crop somewhere…"

Toodles sat next to Tom. Looking at the detective, she explained, "My granddaughter has become a force to be reckoned with."

"I believe we are all here, detective."

He glanced toward the door. When he sat back, he seemed to accept the fact Caro wouldn't be joining them. Certainly not before he divulged every single detail.

"Well," he said. "I'm glad to be able to tell you we have closed the case."

"Indeed."

"We were able to match Archie Arthurs' fingerprints to the partial fingerprint found on the syringe. If you recall, I also had the milk in the stables tested and the examiner found traces of sleeping powder. So, this had been planned to the last detail. Although, as you pointed out, my lady, those involved made the mistake of thinking Sterling Wright wouldn't recognize the different horse."

"Well, that is good news. Did you extract a confession out of him?"

"No, I believe he will maintain his innocence until the end. However, we were lucky to find proof he delivered the fatal blow and, for that, he will face the severest penalty."

"What proof is that?" Henrietta asked.

"Traces of blood on his coat."

Henrietta pressed her hand to her throat. "What about the others? Was Evangeline correct in thinking there were others involved?"

"Up to a point, yes. Marjorie Devon came forward first." The detective looked at Evie. "She was compelled to speak in exchange for clemency for her father who had written those letters to her. He had wanted her to intervene and assist Archie Arthurs in stealing the horse and that is why she provided the information she did." He glanced at Lotte. "She mentioned something about trying to divert attention by suggesting Looney Lotte had sent them. I've searched my mind and tried to recall if you'd mentioned her…"

Evie shrugged. Instead of answering, she turned to Henrietta. "You look confused."

"That's because I am. How did her father become involved?"

"Gambling debts. They were going to sell the horse and he needed the money to pay off his debts."

"And he sacrificed his daughter? That is dreadful." Sara took a sip of her tea and set her cup down. "I have heard say gambling is a disease and drives people to do strange things."

"What about the others?" Henrietta quizzed.

"Mr. Prentiss and Twiggy Lloyd were also involved in an attempt to switch the horse and sell it."

"Will they serve time?"

"That is up to Sterling Wright. He hasn't decided if he will insist on charges being pressed against them. He... He is hesitating because it will force him to involve Marjorie's father and that is something he is reluctant to do as he is determined to continue on with the engagement."

Tom and Evie exchanged a look of surprise.

"My apologies, detective, but I still need clarification."

"Henrietta, what more do you want to know? The man has been caught. That appears to be the end of the story."

"My dear Sara, I am curious about the others. Were they involved in the murder or just the attempt to sell a horse that didn't belong to them?"

The detective glanced toward the door. Sighing, he said, "No, they actually tried to prevent the murder. Apparently, they had been insistent on drawing the line." The detective clasped his hands together. "We did get a small confession out of Archie Arthurs. I noticed he touched his right hand a great deal..."

Before the detective could finish, Evie interjected, "He's the one who hit Caro."

"Yes."

"I wonder... Would it be possible to speak with Lady Carolina?"

Evie tapped her riding crop against her leg. She knew she had made him wait long enough and he had delivered the news as promised. "Edgar, please tell Caro Lady Carolina needs to come down to tea."

The detective shifted to the edge of his seat. "Actually, it's Caro I'd like to see."

Everyone's eyes widened slightly. Even Tom understood the significance. The detective did not harbor any biases against people in service.

The drawing room filled with an air of expectation and excitement.

Moments later, Caro appeared at the door dressed in her neat lady's maid dress. Her cheeks had a light tinge of pink and she only had eyes for the detective.

The detective rose to his feet and invited Caro to accompany him on a walk around the park.

To her credit, Caro did not collapse into the nearest chair. "I'll fetch my coat, detective."

"It's... It's actually Henry."

Caro smiled. "I won't be long, Henry."

The detective turned and gave the others a nervous smile. "Caro is going to fetch her coat."

"Yes, we heard," Sara said and then whispered, "we just can't believe our eyes."

The moment the couple stepped outside, they all rushed to the window to watch them.

"I foresee a short engagement," Sara murmured.

"Let's not get ahead of ourselves," Evie said. "I'll need to contact Inspector O'Neill and ask him about Henry Evans."

Henrietta glanced at Tom. "You should speak with Henry Evans. He might be able to give you a pointer or two on how to get your gal."

When the couple disappeared behind the folly, everyone returned to their chairs and their tea.

"Well," Sara exclaimed, "I daresay, we won't be attending any more functions at Hillsboro Lodge. Sterling Wright might be prepared to forgive Marjorie Devon but I don't believe I can. I hope I speak for everyone."

Evie tried to reason with her. "It would have been a tough choice to make, Sara. It must have been difficult to discover her own father had been willing to use her for his ill-gotten gains. In any case, I wouldn't be surprised if Sterling sells the house and moves on."

After enjoying another cup of tea, Henrietta excused herself saying she had some matters to attend to. Strangely, she needed the others' assistance so Lotte, Sara and Toodles left with her.

"I wonder what that's about?" Evie asked.

"I'm sure you will soon find out." Tom looked around the drawing room. "Listen to that?"

"What?"

"Silence. I wonder how long it will last…"

EPILOGUE

The library
Halton House

"Mr. Winchester. Just the person I wished to see." Henrietta breezed into the library.

Glancing up from her book, Evie noticed Henrietta hadn't come alone. A young man accompanied her. He wore round spectacles and stood a head taller than the Dowager. He had a prominent Adam's apple which bobbed up and down as he adjusted his tie. As he walked, he fidgeted with his tie and nearly collided with Henrietta when she stopped in the middle of the library and tapped her umbrella.

"Everyone, this is Mr. Barclay Chides. He is an expert in genealogy and I have hired him."

Setting her book aside, Evie exchanged a worried look with Tom. "Henrietta. Have you lost your lineage?"

Henrietta chortled. "Sometimes, I do wonder. However, in this instance, I have been in search of someone else's lineage." Henrietta gave Tom a pointed look.

"Do sit down and tell us all about it," Evie invited and noticed Tom hadn't spoken.

Henrietta chose the chair closest to Tom. "You look perplexed."

"Is that how you interpret my look? I'm sure I feel like someone who's been cornered and ensnared."

"Nonsense. Now, we have much work to do and we are going to need your input. When did your people first appear in America?"

"My people?"

"Yes, your forebears." Henrietta's eyes brimmed with excitement. "Mr. Chides believes he can trace your lineage... Oh, but I'm getting ahead of myself and I promised him I wouldn't."

"Oh," Evie exclaimed. "I see it now."

"See what?" Tom asked, his voice filled with caution.

"The cornered and ensnared look."

Tom frowned at her. "Didn't you say we needed to be somewhere else and if we didn't make a start now we'd be late?"

Smiling, Evie sat back. "No, we have nowhere to go."

"Wonderful," Henrietta said. "Let's get started..."

~

Printed in Great Britain
by Amazon

32391868R00144